Princess
FOR HIRE

Princess
FOR HIRE

LINDSEY LEAVITT

SCHOLASTIC INC.
New York Toronto London Auckland
Sydney Mexico City New Delhi Hong Kong

ISBN 978-0-545-33371-9

12 11 10 9 8 7 6 5 4 3 2 1   11 12 13 14 15 16/0

Printed in the U.S.A.   40

First Scholastic printing, January 2011

For Rylee and Talin,
my little princesses

Chapter

I

If my life were made into a movie—*The Desi Bascomb Story Revealed*—I'd use artistic license to make a few minor changes. Like switch the setting to somewhere besides Sproutville, home of the Idaho Potato Days Festival. And rewind back to the forties or fifties, a time of flowing head scarves, glamour, and what's-wrong-with-butter? cuisine. And cast Audrey Hepburn to play me (or a young Julie Andrews if Audrey was on another project). Oh yeah—I'd also give the director some small suggestions, just to add a little sparkle to the otherwise tragic script.

1. Avoid dressing me as a rodent on steroids. There's a reason models aren't sporting groundhog costumes on the catwalk. Actually, make that one

million nine hundred and thirteen reasons, all too gruesome to list.

2. Give me a cooler summer job than passing out goldfish coupons in front of a mall pet store. Literally cooler. Iffy AC + world's worst work "uniform" = stinky, furry sauna.

3. Don't compromise my dignity in the presence of the popular people. Ever.

Basically, avoid portraying my actual life.

But hey. There was one perk to wearing a six-pound groundhog head: while coupon-shoving and toddler-hugging and paw-waving on behalf of Pets Charming pet store, I could stare at anyone in the mall and all they saw was Gladys the Groundhog's permanent smile. So my anguish was perfectly hidden when I spotted the recently crowned Miss Sproutville Spud Princess herself, Celeste Juniper, flirting by the mall fountain with my four-year crush, Hayden Garrison.

Ah, Hayden. My fourth-grade secret online Boggle sweetheart and the cutest boy in Sproutville. Even though he was more than thirty feet away, the heat in my costume shot up a few thousand degrees, which would've happened even in the middle of an Idaho winter. You know the late actor Paul Newman? Way back in the day, before he was on the salad dressing labels, he had this wavy hair with steel blue eyes and a swoonworthy smile, and . . . that's Hayden. Well, a thirteen-year-old version.

Celeste squealed while Hayden rifled through her shopping bags, which, knowing her, were filled with expensive, tacky junk, like DADDY'S PRINCESS T-shirts. Laughing, Hayden dug out a pink feathered purse that had no doubt cost a flamingo its life. When Celeste's glossed lips settled into a pout, Hayden apologized and told her she could pull it off because she was the closest thing to royalty we had at Walter B. Sprout Junior High. She could even wear the purse on her delicate wrist as she waved to the masses lining Main Street for the annual Idaho Potato Days parade tomorrow.

Well, that's probably what he said. It's hard to read lips when you're battling rebellious tear ducts. Plus groundhog heads don't offer much visibility.

I looked away from the lovebirds. Winston, a bull terrier with beady eyes and foul breath, scratched the display glass and whimpered. He'd be graduating from puppy to dog very soon and still hadn't been adopted, poor guy. Sure, he wasn't the cutest doggy in the window, but he had a loyal charm. When he closed his mouth.

"Seriously, Winston. What is Hayden *thinking?*"

He cocked his head in sympathy, then noticed his tail and started chasing it.

I glanced back at the fountain. Oh no. Celeste, with her heart-shaped face and potato-fed freshness (that did not, I should add, match her less than sparkling personality), was headed my way! Any hope for social success next year would shrink to the size of her waist if she discovered me. I'd be lucky to reach school mascot level.

Celeste tapped her finger against the Pets Charming

puppy display window. Hayden jogged up behind her. She leaned into him and sighed, "Aren't they sooooooo cute?"

"Not as cute as you." Hayden instinctively flinched at his own lame line.

If he had said those words to someone else, it could have been sweet. Sweeter still if he was talking to me. I allowed myself a second to pretend he was.

"No, you're cute," I would whisper from behind my locker door in the eighth grade hallway, where Hayden would meet me after every class.

"No, *you* are," Hayden would say, looking sporty and gorgeous in his soccer jersey.

Then I would toss my suddenly bouncy hair and tilt my head at a flirty angle. "We're perfect, aren't we?" I'd ask.

"Yes we are."

"Ex-cuse me?" Celeste interrupted my daydream with a sharp finger snap in my face. Well, in Gladys the Groundhog's face. "Are these puppies for rent?"

"Don't you . . ." I coughed and tried again in a squeakier, hopefully unrecognizable voice. "Don't you mean for sale?"

Celeste rolled her eyes, yet the clumps in her mascara managed to stay put. "No, I mean for rent. For like a month." She scrunched up her nose. "I hate when puppies grow into big, nasty dogs. Like that." She pointed at Winston. "Why can't everything just stay little and cute?"

What an ageist load of bunk. Winston could totally hear her! If only he could breathe on her. "Umm . . . no. We only *sell* puppies," I said. "No rentals, though you might want to try Toy Warehouse. I hear they got a new shipment of Mr. Potty Puppies. Mr. Potty Puppy never turns into a dog. But he never gets potty trained either."

Hayden's laugh came out in staccatoed tsk-tsks.

Celeste chewed her bottom lip. "You're just cranky because you're stuck in that stupid chipmunk costume that isn't even long enough, and your job stinks."

"Chipmunk? It's a groundhog," I said too loudly, my anger getting in the way of my judgment. "Don't you know your rodents?"

"Rodents? Hmmm. You remind me of someone."

Oh no. I tugged my head on tighter and turned toward Winston, like hiding Gladys's face could possibly save me at that moment.

"This pathetic girl who's always trying out for the school plays, but of course she never makes it because she's just too . . . awkward. Know her?" She glanced at Hayden, then pinned her eyes back on me. "We call her Ditzy."

My face burned behind Gladys's smile. Desi. My name is Desi. And you know that, Celeste. Or you did, back when we were best friends. Back in elementary school when we had Alfred Hitchcock marathons and accidentally dyed each other's hair orange and read our darkest secrets to each other and buried them in my backyard. Before you won a beauty pageant and turned into Princess Popular.

Before you completed Operation Crush Desi's Heart by going after Hayden.

"Wait, who's this?" Hayden asked.

Never mind. NOW my heart is officially crushed.

Celeste tossed her highlighted curls. "You know her. She makes her own T-shirts that say stupid things no one understands just so she can prove she's smart. Big forehead . . ." Celeste sneered at my shoes. "Big feet."

Oh man, oh man. Please don't do this. Please don't embarrass me in front of Hayden. Send me to the stocks if you have to. Bleach my hair orange again. But leave Hayden out of this.

"Oh yeah." Hayden yawned. "Her shirts are cool. Daisy."

"How do you know Desi?" Celeste asked.

"Desi. Right. We sit by each other in English. I copy off her paper sometimes." Hayden stuck his hands into the pockets of his blue Bermuda shorts. "Let's go. I wanna get a smoothie."

Yeah, one more poke in my barely beating heart. Copy? I tutor! So maybe sometimes I get frustrated when he doesn't get it, and just hand over my paper. But he plays soccer like EVERY night, and that has to be exhausting. And it's only for big tests. And quizzes. Some work sheets . . .

Didn't someone once say copying is the highest form of flattery?

"Yummy. A smoothie." Celeste smacked her gum. "And thanks for your help. Oops, it looks like your head is crooked."

I grabbed the groundhog head. "No, it's fine. Er . . . thanks."

"Let me just . . ." Celeste yanked it off, confirming my

identity. Steam poured out of the suit. My hair stuck to my face. Tears stung my eyes.

Celeste blew a tropical fruit–scented bubble in my face. It popped, just like my hopes for eighth grade.

Hayden kindly shifted his gaze to Winston. "Whatever, Celeste. I'm getting a drink." He gave me a quick nod of acknowledgment, like *that* helped right now, and headed to the Smoothie Shack a few shops down.

I wanted to scream at Celeste. To ask her how someone who used to be so nice could act so cruel. Tell her that for a teen princess, she had zippo class. But all I got out was, "Why?"

"Wait for me," she called to Hayden. "Oh. Here's your dome back, Ditzy." Celeste shoved the head against my chest. "Guess being a rat runs in the family."

Chapter
2

$\mathcal{I}$ would have walked out right then, but I'm not a quitter. I'm actually more of a crier. I hid by the reptile tanks and let it flow.

A rat. How clever. It's true, Celeste's cruelty wasn't completely random. The summer before seventh grade, my dad, the newly appointed Fredonia County prosecuting attorney (big title, little pay), argued the court case that landed Celeste's dad in jail. Forget that her dad was defrauding people on fake land sales, or even that my dad was just doing his job. Forget that her dad got out in no time and was now enjoying early retirement in the Bahamas. Forget that her mom had filed for divorce even before her dad got caught, then remarried the richest cattle guy in three counties. Celeste was done with me and convinced our whole group of friends that they were too. Maybe farm living had seeped into everyone's brains, making them think like sheep. *Bah.* Follow Celeste. Shun Desi! *Baaahhh!*

I wiped my nose on my fuzzy sleeve. I know it's shallow, but right then I really wished we were rich. Rich girls don't have to dress as rodents for their college money or, as Dad says, "to build moral character." No sooner had the state passed the "Idaho Future Leaders Apprenticeship Program"—which basically legalized child labor—than my dad got me an application for eligibility. Because I'd be turning fourteen in a couple of months, I qualified. Farewell, childhood.

I tried to get a job at Cunningham Horse Stables, picturing myself all Katharine Hepburn–esque as I groomed the purebred horses. But when I showed up for the group interview, half a dozen girls in expensive equestrian gear literally gasped at my specially made (and super cute, what's their deal?) HOLD YOUR HORSES T-shirt. It wasn't a big shocker that they never called me back.

After that (and my failure to convince Dad to invest in screen printing supplies for my struggling T-shirt design business), I had a choice. Either dig up bait worms to sell for two bucks a pound, or comb Sproutville for places that were A) hiring, and B) participated in the new child labor program. Which narrowed it down to one.

Pets Charming. In the aquarium across from my little hiding spot, two dime-priced goldfish bobbed stiffly, dead. Above them, hamster wheels spilled from a sagging cardboard box. The snake staring at me from a cracked tank was one shed skin away from joining the floating fish in pet store heaven. And I, Gladys the Groundhog, wept for us all.

"Okay, take your break." My manager, Drake, sighed and pointed to the back room.

"Why?"

"Look at you. You're scaring the snakes."

I trudged to the back of the store, and Drake followed. It only added to my pain that a twenty-five-year-old high school dropout with unintentional dreads and a distinct catnip odor questioned my work ethic.

"I'm fine, Drake." I tugged off the head. "Sometimes this suit just . . . gets to me."

"Hey, it was the best costume I could find online. I mean, besides the gorilla. But I figured that would scare the kids. If only they'd had a decent chicken—"

"I just . . . Isn't there a way I can do something more proactive?"

Drake poked through the employee fridge and popped open a Mountain Dew. "Tell you what. Stick it out a little bit longer and maybe at the end of the summer we could discuss moving you up to Fish Tank Cleaner."

I knew he was trying to be nice but . . . Fish Tank Cleaner? Spend the next two months pushing coupons and *maybe* I'd be upgraded to Pond Scum Engineer. Yeah, living the life of glamour. Big Idaho dreaming.

"Thanks. But that's not really what I meant."

Drake sighed. "I know. All right." He moved closer and flicked off the lights. "You're obviously having a hard day, so I'm gonna show you something special."

Uh . . . they'd warned us about this in the employee orientation video. "Look, Drake, I don't feel comfortable with you . . . uh . . ."

He didn't say anything for minute, just stared at me funny before bursting into laughter. "You thought . . . Oh, come off it. You're way too young for me. Really, a fetus. Besides, you're not my type. I mean, you're too tall and skinny and I usually like a little meat—"

"I get the point."

Drake flipped on another light. The fish tank in the break room glowed. "But seriously. Look. This is what I wanted you to see."

"It's a fish tank."

"Dude. Look again."

I stepped closer. I'd never thought about it until then, but it was kind of weird that Drake kept a fish tank in here, where customers couldn't see it. It was decked out with all the creature comforts—a treasure chest, cottage, neon plastic seaweed, and a waving SpongeBob figurine. The fish were unique too, iridescent with neon stripes snaking through their fins. The purplish-blue light pulsed right through them.

"It's a wishing tank." Drake sprinkled fish food with reverence.

"Um . . ."

"Believe it. It's true."

I scooted away. The only thing worse than being alone in a cramped room with a skeeze is being alone with a wacko. "What? What makes you think—"

"It works? Easy. We'd just gotten these fish in, special delivery from Guam. And I was feeding them, thinking how much I'd like a girl from Guam, or"—Drake rubbed his nose—"um . . . any girl, really, when this hot chick walks into the store, shopping for a dog."

"And?"

"And I helped her buy one. And got her number. I mean, I never called it—she was too hot to be real—but I keep it in my wallet."

"Point?"

"Dude, *obviously* she was my wish come true. So I bought the fish myself. And it's changed my life. I've got an interview for head manager coming up. And my band booked three gigs last week at Antonio's Pizza. It would have been four, but Thursday is karaoke night."

"If they're so special, why are they in the break room?"

"I can't take them home because I don't trust my roommate." He shivered. "Sushi eater."

I kneeled down and pressed my face against the tank. "How does it work?"

"Well." Drake scratched his head. "I don't know exactly. I feed them and make a wish. But since they just ate . . ." Drake fished a handful of tank rocks out of the pocket of his black jeans. "You can try these. It might only work for me, I don't know."

"Thanks." I picked a few rocks from his outstretched hand. "I mean, yeah, maybe I'll try it out later. If I think of it. Now, if it's okay, I'd like to use the bathroom before my break ends."

Drake paused in the doorway. "All right. But I want you smiling when you get back to work. People can sense your smile, you know, even behind the suit."

I rolled my eyes. "Uh-huh."

"And hey, do you still want to pick up some extra hours at the parade tomorrow?"

I had not once, in my six weeks of employment, passed up an extra shift. An extra shift could buy five blank T-shirts. "Can I do something besides wear this suit?"

"Sure. I told my brother—he works for the city—I'd hook him up with some extra horse . . . shovelers."

"You mean pooper-scoopers."

"Yeah."

Of course. "I'll have to give it some thought."

Drake nodded solemnly and closed the door.

I squeezed the rocks. A wish tank. Oh boy. I'd always wondered if Drake was on some kind of drugs, and now my suspicions had been confirmed. Although, the chances of Drake's luck changing without cosmic intervention were slim. I'd heard his band. They stunk.

I stared at my reflection in the fish tank and pushed my ash brown hair away from my still-blotchy face. Maybe I should cut bangs to cover up the big forehead I didn't even know I had until Celeste so kindly pointed it out. I needed to get rid of the braces too, but I still had ten months to go, and eighth grade started in two. And I only had thirty-six dollars in my non-college savings account—hardly enough to give my wardrobe a much-needed shot of glam. Even if I looked like Audrey Hepburn, which I *so* don't, next year was not going to be much easier than the last.

Thanks to Celeste's sabotage, I was a social bottom feeder. She made her life this big sob story, lied and told everyone I'm evil and a backstabber and who knows what else. And everyone believed her because she's Celeste.

And I've always been kind of different anyway. I don't try to be, I just am. I listen to big band music instead of country, watch old movies instead of MTV. But even more, I've always felt like there was this . . . pulse, this *bigness* in me, like I'm permanently hyped up on caffeine or sugar. The buzzing grew and dimmed with my moods, but the feeling was always *there*.

I guess that's why I was anticipating this next year so much. It was a chance for a fresh start. But that would all be spoiled now that Celeste was probably texting everyone my new nickname, something epically unoriginal like Ditzy the Chipmunk Girl.

A fish stared at me from inside its little fish cottage. Magic. I wanted to believe it, if only until my break ended and my groundhog head went back on, a weighty reminder of who I was.

Or wasn't.

Because I was vapor. Can you get any more invisible than that? Well, I guess complete nothingness would trump vapor, because vapor is still a state of matter. But it's a gas. It floats around, dispersing everywhere and nowhere. It's not a solid.

It makes no impact.

"Impact," I said in as solid a manner as I could muster. It was a modest enough desire—not a new pony or a million dollars. Just to be that girl that others wanted to be around. To be seen with. To know. "I wish I was the kind of person who made an impact. Like Grace Kelly. Minus the car wreck."

It was stupid, but I snuck a blue rock into the water and glanced at the closed door. All the old Hollywood starlets had it. You watch those movies even now, and their magnetism fills the screen. I mean, even a girl in Idaho decades later understands the last look Ingrid Bergman gave Bogie in *Casablanca*. So much in just a look.

If that's not impact, I don't know what is.

"Well?" I asked the fishes.

In response, they kept on swimming. One snatched some lingering fish food from the surface.

And nothing else happened. Obviously.

I was still vapor.

"Desi!" Drake called. "I think some of the cats are sick. Grab some paper towels and cleaner."

I glanced at the remaining rocks in my hand. "And if

I don't get the impact part, I could at least use a more glamorous job."

I gave the rest of the rocks one more squeeze and dropped them in. A fish smiled from the doorway of its sparkly, green castle. Can fish smile? Man, I was losing it. A flurry of green bubbles escaped from the castle tower, floating to the top until they pop, pop, popped.

Chapter
3

What I love about my dad: when he picked me up from work that afternoon, he took one look at my still-puffy eyes, and without saying a thing, drove straight to Taco Bell and ordered me two burritos and a gordita with extra baja sauce.

What I don't love so much:

"How was work? Did you listen to your boss? Prove yourself to be a model employee? Did I ever tell you I was Employee of the Region at the shoe store I worked at in high school?"

"You've mentioned it once or twice." Or every day. Why does my dad always have to go off on his values like that, especially when I'm obviously upset and the last thing I want to discuss is my future employment goals? It made my burrito taste like shoes.

"So?" Dad eased out of the drive-through, his hands at the ten and two position. He's the only person I know who actually follows the school speed zones. When school is already out for the summer. Just in case.

I shoved some gooey, beany goodness into my mouth and shrugged. "So what?"

"Either you're allergic to your groundhog suit, or you've been crying. Bad day?" Worry flashed across his face. "You didn't get into any sort of trouble, did you?"

"Work was fine. Thanks for asking."

"Well then, what's wrong, Princess?"

"Please don't call me that, Dad."

"What? Princess? But you've always been my princess." Dad stopped at a yellow light. The car behind us swerved and honked. He turned around and waved. "What is everyone's hurry these days?"

I squirted some hot sauce onto my gordita. "I'm not a princess, all right? More like the palace stable cleaner. I wear a groundhog suit and my forehead is big and Celeste Juniper is such a . . . Basically, I'm vapor—"

"Vapor? Desi, what are you *talking* about? You don't really think of yourself like that, do you?"

"Sometimes," I admitted.

"First off, you are the most solid girl I know. And I'm sorry you're experiencing fallout from that trial, but convicting Celeste's very guilty dad was the right thing to do. It's sad his choices negatively impacted his family, and, I guess, you too. But *I* didn't have a choice. I had to do my job. I had to

18

do what was right. You can understand that, can't you?" The light turned green and Dad resumed his careful navigation of the only six-lane street in town.

I did understand. But no one else seemed to. It reminded me of a poster my history teacher had hanging up in her classroom that said "What is right is not always popular, and what is popular is not always right."

You know what? I should design a new T-shirt tonight. BEING RIGHT IS <u>OVERRATED</u>.

After we got home, I ran upstairs with the intent to veg. Like, go into a coma, although that wouldn't be much different from my job, because standing around in a costume is like doing a zombie impersonation anyway. Mom had gone *compulsive* on my room. After digging my design sketches out of the trash, I unmade my bed and kicked at the carpet's perfect vacuum lines, my small attempt to make my room look inhabited, because that is the *point* of a bedroom.

After I arranged my pillows into a perfect heap, I switched on my favorite movie, *Roman Holiday*, about a princess who takes a day off. Amazing movie, except for the end, which makes me cry, so I always turn it off early and invent a better ending, usually with more kissing. Anyway, while Audrey Hepburn rode a Vespa through the streets of Rome (tough life, right?), I flipped through my new issue of *Teen Vogue*: The Royals Edition. There was a delicious picture of Prince Barrett of Fenmar in there, although it would be hard for him not to look delicious with his long and lean body, Scandinavian features, and self-assured smile. I cut it out and added it right next to an old shot of a shirtless Paul Newman on my Wall O' Awesome Things. I liked to mix some new pics with old *Life* magazine covers I found online. It took up half my wall and drove my mom NUTS.

When I'd had enough daydream therapy, I picked up the phone to invite my friend Kylee Malik to my whine-and-cheese party (hold the cheese).

"Desi! Oh my gosh. I'm so glad you called," she said in one excited breath.

"Hey to you too. Why are you so giddy?"

"There's a new boy! From New Zealand. In Sproutville. His name's Reed, and he's a year older. My mom talked to his mom at the farmers' market. They're here for some agricultural research thing. But, Desi. You have to see him."

"Did you talk to him?"

"Not yet. Actually, I only saw him from far away because I was at the tomato stand, but if his up-close matches his far-away, then there will be much call to rejoice. Like, hallelujah-angels-singing rejoice."

"Oh, well, congratulations."

"Congratulations? Okay, you aren't excited enough. What's wrong?"

"Nothing. Well, sort of. It's . . . it's Hayden."

"Oh. Hayden."

"I saw him today." My voice cracked. "With Celeste. And Celeste took my head off and . . . and . . ." I choked back the tears. "And Hayden saw me in that stupid groundhog costume, and now I have no chance. Plus, Miss Teen Queen Idaho is going to totally blab about this and next year will be even worse than the last two. Seriously, I wish you could have seen his face when she de-headed me. I'm done."

"All right. Deep breaths. You can get through this."

I tried to smile through the hysterics. Kylee and I had only started hanging out when she'd made a joke in English about *West Side Story* and no one laughed but me. She'd always intimidated me a little—she's super witty and practically a master clarinetist. Plus, she lived in Seattle until last year, which automatically upped her coolness factor. Her parents are from India, and in a town as white as Wonder Bread, she's too different for the high-maintenance girls (or HMs, as we call them). Unlike me, though, she'd rather eat Winston's dog chow than hang out with them.

Anyway, I kind of mentioned I liked Hayden one day, and once it was out and I actually had someone to talk to, I couldn't stop. But she'd listen, so I hoped next year we'd break into that next level of friendship—where everyone refers to us as "KyleeandDesi," and we can't wait to tell each other about every life detail. It'd been forever—well, two years to be exact—since I'd had that.

I hiccupped and waited for her pity.

"First off, I want you to know that I think you're a great, caring person. In fact, sometimes I think you care *too* much."

Dear sweet Kylee.

"Second, I want a real answer, all right?"

"Um . . . what?"

"Okay, so I don't want this to sound rude, and I hope we're tight enough that I can say this without hurting you, but really—why do you even like Hayden? Is it just because he's hot? I mean, yes, he's very, very cute, but he's not really a match for you, you know? He's totally into sports and not really nice and, well, he seems kind of . . . stupid."

Stupid? What happened to dear sweet Kylee? "Hayden's not stupid! He's a word person like me. He plays Boggle. Boggle players have . . . depth. And he *is* nice, just a quiet kind of nice. Like he lets his friends cut him in the lunch line. And today, *today* he said he liked my T-shirt designs."

"But is that enough to keep a million-year crush going? To be honest, Des, this Hayden thing is a waste of my phone minutes, and it's a waste of your life."

"This isn't a *thing* with Hayden. It's an . . . an investment. And I really, really like him."

I could almost hear Kylee roll her eyes over the phone.

"Get real. You need a new guy. A guy like Hayden Garrison will never stop admiring himself long enough to notice you. You're sweet, smart, and hilarious. You deserve better."

It was fine for *me* to say this, but way out of line for Kylee to dismiss my potential soul mate as a *thing*. "Sorry I said anything," I said, clearly not sorry.

"I'm just trying to help you," Kylee said.

"Just forget it, okay?"

"Hey, I am! And if you can't see that, then I'm the one who's sorry."

I didn't answer. The silence turned brutal. Months and

months of delicate progress erased in two awkward minutes.

"I have to go," Kylee said.

"Me too."

"Uh-huh."

"I'll see you tomorr—"

"Bye." *Click.*

Forget making an impact. Thanks to my big mouth, I was doomed to a solitary life of bottom-feeding dorkdom. I trudged to the bathroom, dumped half a bottle of bubble bath into the tub, and tried not to think about the day's disasters. In a hot bath, surrounded by bubbles, I could almost picture myself at a spa with celebrity magazines—no, actual celebrities!—where my biggest problem would be picking a massage package, not strategizing ways to erase the Groundhog Debacle from my crush's memory. Or wondering if I'd ever make a best friend again.

I let the tub fill while I wandered downstairs to get the newspaper. I needed to find a new job and fast.

In the kitchen, Mom held Gracie on her hip while she stirred a bowl of organic baby food. It freaked me out how much my mom and sister looked alike, especially because the only maternal physical trait I'd inherited was a double-jointed thumb. They both wore pink sundresses; Gracie's auburn hair was pulled into pigtails and Mom's was twisted up.

No one bought me a matching sundress, not that I'd wear it, especially a pink one. Not my style. But it would've been nice if Mom had, you know, offered.

The newspaper was on the kitchen counter, along with a letter from another pageant organization. Mom was Miss Idaho in college, and she also taught charm classes in our formal living room, a course I failed ("Watch the crumbs, dear. Pinkie up! Don't frown, you'll get wrinkles") while whiz kid Celeste flew through to her first pageant win.

"They want you to MC another one?" I nodded toward the letter.

Mom smiled her perfect didn't-even-need-braces-guess-it-was-just-good-genes smile. "Yes, but I think I'll have to decline. I need to strengthen my connection with Gracie, so we're enrolling in a Mommy and Me sculpting class."

"You know Gracie isn't even two yet, right?"

"She's a toddler. Much of who you become as a person is decided in those early years."

"What was I like as a toddler?" I stuck my finger into the baby food. Bananas.

Mom slapped my hand. "Stubborn, but in a good way. When you were eight months, you decided you wanted to walk. It took you two months and lots of falling to get it, but you never quit. I always thought you'd change the world."

I swallowed. *Thought.* Past tense.

"So what happened at work today?" Mom asked. "Dad said you were pretty upset."

"Oh, nothing. My boss believes his fish tank has mystical powers, and Celeste . . . came by the store."

"I hope you weren't mean to her, honey. I feel so bad for everything she's been through."

I collapsed against the counter. Everything *she'd* been through? Yes, being a nasty HM can be quite exhausting. "Mom, you don't know what she's like."

"Don't slouch, honey."

I automatically rolled my shoulders back.

She smoothed a hair out of my face. "Now, you're not going to believe this, but I've been there too."

"Uh, sure you have."

My mom was voted best personality, had a boyfriend every year since she was twelve, and had probably never even gotten a zit. Her version of "there" wasn't even in the same galaxy as mine.

"It's true. I was very close friends with this girl until sixth grade. Then I developed sooner and she started spreading cruel rumors about me. It's just jealousy."

"This isn't the same. You don't see it. Like, there's this boy—"

"Ba!" Gracie said.

"Oh my gosh!" Mom laughed.

"What?"

"Jeremy, get in here. Gracie stuck her hand in the baby food and called it 'ba'! She knew it was a banana!"

Dad zipped in with the video camera just in time to catch Gracie flicking a glob onto Mom's dry-clean-only dress, and he and Mom squealed their encouragement.

"She's brilliant!" Dad kissed Gracie's chubby cheek. "And the camera loves her already!"

"She does have *presence*," Mom added with pride.

Gracie held out a pudgy, mush-covered hand to me.

I stroked her cheek, glad someone was including me. My parents didn't even notice when I snatched the newspaper and left them to plan my little sister's future.

When I got upstairs, the bathwater was close to overflowing. I turned off the faucet and stepped into the tub, making sure to keep my hands and newspaper dry.

Heaven.

Well, about ten seconds of heaven before I remembered why I needed to relax. I flipped to the personals first (hey, what did I have to lose at this point?), but all the self-titled Prince Charmings were divorced and fifty. Besides, I'd liked Hayden ever since he'd given up his swing for me in fourth grade. Saw my need and chivalrously left. Granted, he'd run over to the drinking fountain, then wanted the swing back, but that noble act had proven to me that he was Paul Newman and more. And, okay, his looks played a part. A tiny part.

I flipped to the classifieds page. Ads looking for everything from models to receptionists to library janitors. Maybe I'd find an advertisement for a ridiculously tall teenaged girl with mascot experience. Maybe I could pick apples or pull things off people's shelves.

On the next page, one ad popped out instantly. Among the tiny black-and-white posts, this one was written in green loopy cursive and took up half a page. In fact, it was so blinding, I almost dropped the paper in the tub. What kind of ink had they used? For a second, I swore the words *shimmered*.

Perfect. The ad was far from specific, but I figured they
wanted someone to dress up. Do some parties. Wave a wand
and make little girls giggle. I could do that. A princess
costume beats the heck out of rodent-wear. And a poofy
dress would cover up my bird legs. Show off my waist. Ooh,
maybe I'd get a tiara and a wig. A blond bob like Marilyn
Monroe! Then I wouldn't care if Hayden Garrison saw me at
work. In fact, I'd be ecstatic for Hayden to see me in that
getup.

Plus, I'd always secretly had this thing for princesses.
Think of it. Ordinary girls, like Cinderella, who have all
these great qualities no one notices except the mice. Or
Sleeping Beauty, who is fair and pure and doesn't even know
she's a princess! Snow White—well, Snow White kind of
confuses me, actually—but even ol' Snow is able to escape
from laundry duty. Sure, the stories aren't exactly feminist
battle cries, but still it's sweet how the prince just knows she's
the one. And after that, *everything* changes, everything is
wonderful, and the girl goes from a nobody to the biggest
somebody in the kingdom.

Who wouldn't want that?

The fantasy was short-lived. The ad didn't even have a contact number! All it said was "Please call Meredith."

Why would they use such expensive ink and not even leave a number or last name?

Lame.

"Hey, Meredith! Take this!" The newspaper fluttered as it sailed across the room. I slid under the bubbles, holding my breath until I couldn't take it anymore.

When I sat up, head swimming, the bubbles floated around me. One bubble rose out of the bath toward the ceiling. It hung in the air and began to grow. I rubbed my eyes, thinking the bath soap had blurred my vision.

It hadn't. The bubble was now the size of a watermelon, and blooming by the second. I jumped out of the tub as the bubble neared the size of a yoga ball. Water sloshed onto the floor. My heart hammered.

Obviously, the groundhog costume fumes caused hallucinations. I wondered if my dad would count insanity as an excuse for me to quit. Probably not.

I wrapped myself in my towel and backed away from the soapy apparition. It grew until there wasn't any room left. Then . . .

Pop!

The bubble burst. Soap splattered the walls, and foam covered my face. I fumbled for a hand towel, wiped off the suds, and screamed.

I was not alone in the bathroom.

Chapter
4

"Calm down!" said a low, clipped voice. "Human eardrums were not meant for sounds that loud. And jaws were not meant to drop that low." The woman standing in front of me shut my gaping mouth with one long finger. "If we're going to work together, your manners will need serious help."

The short woman, dressed in a black pinstriped business suit and open-toed heels, placed her hand on her hip. The only thing stronger than her citrusy perfume was her air of importance. Everything about her was sophisticated, from her creamy brown skin to her perfectly plucked eyebrows and sharp features. She looked like she'd arrived straight from a fashion runway, except for one thing. Her hair was a shocking shade of chartreuse green.

It took me a few moments to find my voice post-scream. "Why . . . why are you in my bathroom?" I clutched the towel even closer to my dripping skin. Who was this woman, and how had she floated in that bubble like Glinda from *The Wizard of Oz*? Most important, why was she here, with me? Had I drowned?

"Darling, there's no need for modesty." Still, she kicked my clothes across the room and turned around.

I took that as my cue to throw on my shirt and tug my jeans onto my still-wet legs. If I had drowned (or maybe I was in the process of drowning and this was an in-between-being-alive-and-dead hallucination?), at least my parents wouldn't have to fish me out of the tub naked. Although, if I was drowning, how was I standing up?

"How did you—"

"Are we playing the question game here?" She twisted back toward me, her heels clicking on the tile. "I don't have time. Take note. Only ask what you really need to know. You're not my only client. People to see, things to do. Although we might have time for an emergency makeover. What a hideous shirt. What does it say?"

I fingered the tiny red print running along the middle of my navy T-shirt. FLOCCINAUCINIHILIPILIFICATION.

She eyed the bathroom warily. "The places they send me. Is that some Idaho thing?"

"It's the longest real word in the English language. It means estimating something as worthless. So I made the letters small, like they don't matter. It's a great word, right? I design my own T-shirts on my computer, and try to make them ironic or funny. I do other kinds of graphic design too—pamphlets and Web site banners, but I just got this new T-shirt computer program, so I mostly focus on that. If you want, I have a Web site—"

"Well, aren't you a little chatterbox?"

Her question cut into my fevered marketing pitch and snapped me back to reality—if having a strange woman pop out of a bubble can be considered reality. "I'm sorry, but, uh . . . who *are* you?"

"Fine." The woman's smile looked pained. "We're on a tight schedule so I'd hoped to skip the formalities. But here they are. I'm Meredith Pouffinski. Princess agent extraordinaire, or so I've been told."

I blinked. She blinked. I blinked again.

"Now would be the time for you to say your name. It's a complicated practice, introductions. I hope you can make it through this."

She was insulting me. In my bathroom! Wait, why in the world was she popping up in my *bathroom*?

"Uh, Desi." I cleared my throat. "I'm Desi."

"Desi. Hmm . . ." She tapped her dimpled chin. "That doesn't work for me. What is Desi short for?"

"Nothing. Just Desi."

"How about Despina? Greek for *young lady*. I like that better."

Wow. This couldn't be a dream because I'd have come up with someone a whole lot more bippity boppity booish than this lady. This was headed in the direction of a nightmare.

"Okay, wait." I pushed on my temples. Everything in the room, Meredith's annoyed expression in particular, was remarkably clear. Aren't hallucinations supposed to be all fuzzy? "So why are you here exactly?"

She was taken aback. "Excuse me? Remember, I got a call from *you*."

"What?"

"Right there in the ad: Call Meredith. And you did. Now I'm here. Only girls with some Magic Potential can see the ad." She peered at my dripping hair. "Though mistakes have been known to happen."

"How did you get here?"

"That big round thing you saw floating around? It's called a bubble."

"I know, but *how?*"

"The bubble lifts off the ground." Meredith spoke slowly, pantomiming the bubble's actions. "It floats to where I want it to go. It lands."

I chose to ignore her sarcasm. "Okay. So you're magical or something. Are you a witch?"

She laughed. "Don't I wish. Witches get all the press, don't they? No, as I said, I'm an agent based in Europe. I book princess gigs for young girls like yourself while the real princesses go on their escap—er . . . vacations."

"So you're real. I'm not dreaming or drowning. You . . . I . . . we're alive."

She seized my arm, pinching until her nails broke my skin. "Feel alive now?"

"Ow! All right." I breathed out. I was breathing. I had to be alive. Bruiser Agent Lady was very much real. But was she *for* real? "If you're an agent, then I'd be, like, a pretend princess? That was a real ad in the paper?"

"Do you think I have a high enough salary to run fake ads? Have you seen how much they're charging per word these days? Ridiculous." She ran her hands along the laminate sink and shook her head when she saw Mom's lace-edged hand towels. "The reason you were able to see the ad is because of your MP. Magic Potential. See, magic lives in organic things. Trees, birds . . . fish. Those fish in your store come from an unpolluted reef, thus their MP is stronger. Industrialization, pollution, deforestation—basically all human activity—has lessened the amount of magic left in the world."

"What does that have to do with princesses?" I asked.

"Getting there." She glared. "Now, humans have the capacity to house magic also, though it's become increasingly rare, thanks to environmental toxins, food preservatives, reality TV, and who knows what else. So for our inner magic to ignite, we need to interact with another magical organism. When you made a wish on those fish, it triggered your magic, which sent a signal to our agency. We in turn ran a check on your MP via the ad. You found it, so here I am offering a position. Presto."

"So I have magic?"

"Have you ever tried to fly with fairy dust?"

"Yes . . ."

"Were you over the age of ten?"

I ducked my head. "Uh, yeah, but—"

"Then you are a dork. A dork with MP. Look, you probably believed in nonsense like unicorns forever, and feel things really, really strongly. Beyond what's normal for a hormonal teenager even. It's a part of the natural energy inside you."

I tried to stop myself from shaking. This, whatever THIS was, might actually be happening. To me. I couldn't argue the proof—I'd seen the bizarre ad. The ballooning bubble. The pinching princess agent. The boiling bigness inside me.

So what if . . .

This moment was magical. I, Desi the Vapory Groundhog Bascomb, was . . . magical.

Yeah, right.

But what a fabulous dream I was having. I decided to play along. "You're giving me a job working with royalty? And I don't have to dress like a groundhog?"

"Job's yours, and yes, your clients—my clients—are royal. But I can't promise anything on the groundhog front. You never know which way styles will go."

"How long do I work? I mean, what are the hours like?"

"Short term—you work until the job is done." She shrugged. "Could be a day, could be a week. It's no nine to five."

"But my family's going to wonder what's up, you

know, when I never come down from my bath, right?"

"Don't worry about your family. When you've completed each shift with the agency—however long that ends up being—I'll return you home a millisecond later than when you left."

"That isn't possible."

"Duh. Law of Duplicity. Think of the time you're working as a piece of string that's stretched out. The magic has the power to bring those string tips together again like that time away never happened, returning you to the tub, dreaming about Boggle Boy."

"I still don't . . . Wait. How do you know about Boggle Boy?"

She scowled at her watch. "Wow. Look at the time. Is it really that late? I have to make some calls. So are you in or out?"

Was I in? In-SANE. There was a lady with green hair making a job offer in my bathroom. "I have to decide right now?"

Meredith whipped out a piece of pale lavender paper. "Here's your contract. Don't worry, it's legit. As you can see, I get a twenty-five percent cut. Nonnegotiable. Your first gig is probationary. You may have Magic Potential, but it remains to be seen if you have *Princess* Potential. So training comes after the final phase of screening, which is unpaid. We have you sign the contract now for liability purposes."

The song "Someday My Prince Will Come" filled the room, and Meredith flipped open an expensive-looking cell

35

phone. "I've got to take this. Read it over. Decide." She turned her back to me and started yapping in turbo speed.

RULES AND REGULATIONS OF FAÇADE AGENCY
(And all subsidiaries therein and thereof and . . . therewith)

I, the undersigned, do hereby agree to all the rules and regulations hitherto mentioned and know that if any of these rules are broken, I not only risk terminating my position, but may also face the Court of Royal Appeals and suffer any sentence dished out. (If the title sounds like a big deal, that's because it is. You don't want to find out how big of a deal. I mean, we're not the devil, your soul is safe. But that's about it. Follow the rules.)

1. I will not reveal my true identity to anyone, on any job. under any circumstance. ANY circumstance.

2. I will also not tell anyone in my real life about my job. (Like they'd believe you.)

3. I will not act contrary to the nature of the client and will respect who they are as a person, spoiled brats included, by addressing situations as I believe the client would.

4. I will keep my clients out of the tabloids.

4a. Unless they LIKE being in the tabloids.

5. Time off, salary, and benefits will be settled privately and verbally with my agent before the contract is finalized. Otherwise, all specifics may be interpreted however the agent sees fit.

6. I will not damage any property of FAÇADE, specifically

36

the bubbles. The only loophole would be extreme conditions where my life is in mortal danger, and that is a very small loophole.

   *And, of course, the old fine print warning: We mean business, and can amend any of the rules accordingly. Although, if the above rules are broken, the fine print is the least of your worries.

   We mostly just add it to look more official.

I HAVE READ, UNDERSTOOD, AND ACCEPTED THE ABOVE TERMS AND CONDITIONS OF EMPLOYMENT.

   Signature of Employee: _____

   Date: _____

Meredith flipped her phone shut. "Well?"

I steadied myself against the sink. My arm still throbbed. Meredith's perfume hung in the air. There was a contract in my hand.

Hallucinations and dreams aren't scented. There isn't fine print! This was craziness!

The room started to spin.

Meredith stepped back. "Why are you looking at me like that? You're not going to throw up, are you? Not on these shoes, got it? They haven't even hit stores yet and . . ."

I tuned her out as this thought occurred to me: my inner magic (INNER MAGIC!) and Drake's fish tank had delivered a ticket to ride. If Meredith had arrived in a bubble, that meant, conceivably, I could leave in the bubble with her. And go . . . places.

Big, non-Idaho places.

"Let me see if I'm a hundred percent here. You want me to get into a bubble and travel to *other countries* so I can stand in for *princesses* while they're on *vacation?*"

Meredith tapped the wall of the bathroom. "This room has amazing acoustics. I swear it has the loudest echo I've ever heard."

"Funny." I folded my arms. "All right, say I signed this contract. Can we go over condition five? Like, what's the pay?"

She smiled, and this time it reached her eyes. "Now we're talking. Payment depends on the length of the assignment, the difficulty, and your PPRs—Princess Progress Reports. Although, since you are under eighteen and your parents would wonder how you came into the money, we have to find creative ways to deposit it." She waved a hand in the air. "Anyway, it's a complicated point system that factors these things and more, but on average I'd say fifty a gig."

"Fifty dollars?" I made that working a full shift at Pets Charming. "That's not that much."

"Fifty melios, darling. And I don't have the time to explain the exchange rate right now." Meredith released an exasperated breath. "Are you in or out?"

Adrenaline rushed through me. I took the silver pen she held out to me, and paused. My history teacher had another poster on her wall that said "In time of action, most successful leaders don't think, they just do." Or maybe it was they don't do, they just think. Probably an important detail to remember.

I did it. I signed my name.

Meredith snapped her fingers and the contract evaporated. "Done deal. Now the bubble." She pointed her phone in the direction of the tub and pressed a large red button where the logo would normally be. A marble-sized bubble sprang out of the antenna and grew until it took up most of the room.

Meredith stepped halfway through the iridescent green blob without getting any soap on her suit. I placed my hand on the curved exterior but pulled away quickly. What I'd thought would be cool and wet was warm and . . . firm. Firm and real.

My stomach twisted. Everything was going so fast. Didn't I need to sign some tax paperwork first, or take a blood test? Was I supposed to hop through the bubble and just START?

"Wait, now?"

Meredith didn't answer. All she did was give me one fierce look and disappear.

Guess that's a yes. I felt my way along the outside of the wall until I reached the spot where Meredith had vanished. My hand broke through. A doorway. Or entryway. Bubbleway? Whatever. A soothing whoosh surrounded me as I slipped inside.

Chapter
5

On the outside, the bubble was translucent, the kind that emerges from a little kid's bubble wand. Once we were inside, my view of the bathroom disappeared. Now there were four walls, metal bookshelves, a green leather couch, funky chairs, a black lacquered coffee table covered with magazines, and a sleek desk with nothing on it but a high-tech laptop. Meredith's office.

Meredith pressed a button on her remote/cell phone, and the floor rattled. I grabbed the edge of her desk to brace myself for the lifting feeling—like going up in an elevator. Meredith brushed my hand away in annoyance and flipped open her phone. "Pouffinski speaking." She motioned to the couch and swiveled around in her chair so her back was turned. "Darling, it's been ages! I just saw that spread in *Elle*, and I've never seen cheekbones so flawless. Now, tell me. How's my favorite soon-to-be monarch doing?"

I sifted through the magazines and tabloids, swallowing when I realized I could very well be working for one of the faces smiling at me from the glossy pages. The same issue of *Teen Vogue* I'd been reading just that day was in there, and that connection from my real life to whatever parallel universe I'd just entered made me stop shaking some. I mean—just an hour or so ago I was cutting out this same picture of Prince Barrett, and now I might meet him! Or BE one of the many royals he'd dated!

Except when I looked more closely, I realized it wasn't the same magazine. This was thicker, the details more specific. Like, I had no idea Prince Barrett was dating American heiress Floressa Chase, but the collage of pictures proved it. I had thought he was with some English duchess. So why did this magazine have more info? I flipped back to the front. There it was, underneath the title in sparkling italics, *Special Façade printing*.

Worried my head might explode, I put the magazine on my lap and continued eavesdropping on my agent's (my agent's!) conversation.

"October? Well, I'll have to see." Meredith's fingers flew across the laptop keyboard. "Of course, for you I'll make it happen, even if I have to put on a tiara myself." Schmoozey laughter. Air kisses. "You too. Yes, all right. Ta-ta." And she hung up.

"Who was that?"

"That spoiled Chase girl."

"Chase? Who, like, Floressa Chase?"

"Yes. That's the second time she's called—"

"Floressa Chase called you. Floressa Chase, who is like the richest heiress ever and"—I pointed to the spread in front of me—"was spotted in Dubai with Prince Barrett—"

"Yes, she called me. They call, I book, and you work."

"But Floressa isn't a—"

"Royal? Ah, well, we have information even those tabloids do not. Including paternity tests, and—well, let's just say Floressa's status may be changing very soon amid scandal and uproar."

"So I'm going to SUB for her? Wait, I could be Floressa Chase? The same Floressa Chase who is every fashion designer's muse, who *bought* a sports team for her old boyfriend? That is so—and isn't she like sixteen? I can't—"

"Forget about it. Floressa will be Level Two, possibly higher. You still haven't finished your job screening. Now, if you need to go to the bathroom"—she pointed to a door— "this would be a good time."

I walked into the black marble bathroom. I didn't need to use it, so I sat on the toilet seat and collected my thoughts. This was so unreal. Floressa Chase? Real royals? How could I concentrate enough to do whatever I was supposed to do on this probationary job? I had to nail it—I couldn't go back to Sproutville when there was this amazing opportunity! Or know I had MP and not find a way to explore what that meant.

I ran my fingers through my hair, still wet and sticking to the back of my shirt. My FLOCCINAUCINIHILIPILIFICATION T-shirt. Problem: not exactly princess apparel.

Meredith was casually sipping tea when I walked out of the bathroom, my big forehead crinkled with concern.

"Don't worry about your appearance. You won't look like you once we get there."

"Who will I look like?" I asked.

"Madonna," she said. "Oh for heaven's sake, who do you'll think you'll look like? The princess."

"So no one will see the real me?"

"Nope. Thanks to this." Meredith whipped out an antique brass compact from her purse and pushed it into my hands. It had Egyptian-looking hieroglyphics around the edges, and a hippo in the center with large rubies for eyes. Real rubies? "When the jewels change to green, that's your application signal, sent to us by the departing royal. Brush two dabs on each cheek and wait twenty minutes. And make sure you don't overdo it. Too much or too little and the timing gets off."

I wiped my hand on my jeans, took the compact, and opened it slowly. The makeup smelled like coconut and something musky. Using a drugstore-variety brush, I swept some rose-colored powder onto my cheeks. The mirror inside had strange words running across the top—CATTER'S PHYSICAL SPECIFICATIONS—followed by a bunch of random numbers and formulas. A digital clock counted down the twenty minutes. Nineteen minutes and thirty-eight seconds to go. "Is it . . . like pixie dust?"

"Royal Rouge. I know, no one says rouge anymore, but this stuff dates back to ancient Egypt. It transforms your physical appearance, voice, and language. So you'll speak the royal's language but hear English no matter what country you travel to. Now, behavior and assimilation you do on your own. That's what we're testing you on right now."

"But even with all that—this rouge and whatever— don't the royals ever get suspicious someone is using a sub?"

"Look, we've been around for centuries because we're excellent at what we do. My girls have very few Sub Spottings. First off, you look exactly like the princess. Her peers see what they want to see, and that isn't you. Next, we don't issue subs during political drama or big scandals, only for day-to-day life. Because it's an elite and very *personal* service, the princesses pay big bucks for our discretion and otherwise try to pretend we don't exist. Funny enough, most of our clients think they're the only ones in their circle who have the daring to hire us. It's part of the thrill."

"I'm sorry, but I'd think a mom would know when it's not really her daughter."

She nodded. "Sometimes family is aware of sub usage if they're traveling together—say a mother-daughter shopping trip they don't want to clue the king in on. Although you'll only be subbing for girls between twelve and sixteen, we offer subs to high-ranked royal women of all ages. But otherwise, darling, we're just *that good*. Our subs are trained to copy the attitude and behaviors of the princess. Think of yourself as an actress, and being Desi is not in the script."

"So no makeover?"

Meredith stirred her tea. "Don't you worry about that. You'll be made over. Again and again and again."

That elevator feeling, this time going down, came over me until the bubble's movement ended altogether.

"Good. That was uneventful." Meredith stood up and brushed off her tailored suit. "So. We're here."

"Where?"

"You're about to find out."

Chapter
6

I followed Meredith through the open part of the bubble wall, ending up on a tiled bridge in what looked like the courtyard of an old European city. I sucked in a breath. Intricate stone buildings rose above tourists breezing into the expensive shops. Three-tiered lamps lit the square—odd, considering it was daytime. Compared to wide-open Idaho, the cloud-feathered blue sky felt small and intimate. They must've had excellent sanitation workers—there wasn't a pigeon or piece of trash in sight.

A thin boat slid underneath us, guided by a man in a black-and-white-striped shirt and red handkerchief. He opened his mouth and the square filled with his operatic voice. Opera. Italian? Yes! Those boats, the water, the square . . . we were in Venice!

"Oh, poof," Meredith said.

I clapped my hands together. "It's stunning. I . . . I've always wanted to come here!"

Meredith tapped her heels, annoyed. "Really? Kind of tacky to me."

Tacky is my great-aunt Monica arguing cookie prices with Girl Scouts. This place was everything Sproutville wasn't.

A man in plaid shorts and a neon orange fanny pack bumped right into me without apologizing.

"Excuse you," I said.

"He can't see you, Desi. Same with the bubble. Look."

She pointed at the crowds walking through the bubble like it didn't exist. Every so often, someone would stop for a second and look around before moving on. "The people pausing might have enough MP to sense something, but not enough to see the bubble or anything else touched by magic, which includes us at the moment. Now scoot back in. I messed up our entrance. Can't wait to trade in this piece of junk for a model with a built-in navigational system."

"But I—"

Meredith yanked me back inside. "It'll just be a second. I don't feel like walking all the way to the ballroom."

The ballroom. I was about to enter a Venetian ballroom as a princess. And Celeste thought cutting the ribbon at the new senior center was something to brag about. "I can't believe I'm going to a royal ball!"

"A royal ball." Meredith snorted. "Oh, this is going to be good."

The bubble rumbled down. "Now, if there are any emergencies during your trial, like body mutilation or, oh, I don't know, you're kidnapped, there is another sub undercover, watching you. She'll step in and assist if you need it; otherwise, don't worry about her. Just feel assured that there is help nearby, but only for this first gig. I've got another appointment to get to. Check the timer on your rouge."

I opened the compact. "Three minutes."

"Perfect. Don't worry—it doesn't hurt. Take the elevator up to the second floor—that should give you just enough time. Have fun. Wish I could see the look on your face when you enter . . . ha! . . . the ball."

The *ha!* made me pause. Meredith didn't strike me as the type to relish others' happiness. What was so funny?

She dropped me off in a massive hallway. The design here was as detailed as outside—pudgy naked angels flew across the ceiling, and different kinds of molding covered the walls. I tapped the elevator button and bit at a hangnail as the doors closed.

Here we go, you lucky girl. A friendless rodent this afternoon, and now, in one floor, royalty. ROYALTY! A weird prickly sensation spread over my body. Excitement? No, my hand was shrinking. I was shrinking. Changing. The Royal Rouge must be kicking in.

The elevator beeped, taking me up before I'd pushed my floor number. My arms and legs itched, and the skin on my face tightened. I sat down and closed my eyes while the magic pulsed through me. I couldn't watch anymore—it was the freakiest thing I'd ever experienced.

The freakiest thing until the elevator opened on my floor. Because standing in front of me, checking his watch, was a human-sized praying mantis.

I'd always wondered how I'd react when seized by true terror. Turns out I'm a silent screamer—wide open mouth but barely a gurgle. So while I cowered in the corner, gurgling, the praying mantis offered one of his six legs and raised me from the fetal position.

His hand felt . . . human. I rubbed his thumb. Wait, a thumb? Fabric, maybe . . . polyester.

Oh my gosh. It was a *costume*. Meredith hadn't shrunk me or transported me to another dimension via an elevator. It/he wasn't going to eat me. Just escort me.

We must be going to a costume ball! I would have preferred something more dignified than an insect for my royal escort, but given my previous job, I couldn't be too picky.

I exhaled slowly, releasing my frozen scream.

"That good, huh?" The praying mantis's Irish accent did not match his piercing, buggy eyes. "Do you think they made my antennae too stiff? I was supposed to have injured them in the Earwig Skirmish of '84, and these convention fans can sniff a fake through all the casino smoke."

"Ear . . . Earwig?"

Something was wrong. Conventions and casinos

49

don't mesh with ballrooms and masquerades.

Behind Praying Mantis Guy, a large banner hung over a doorway. THE LAS VEGAS VENETIAN HOTEL PROUDLY PRESENTS THE 28TH ANNUAL NATIONAL MUTANT INSECT BATTALION CONVENTION. MEET PRINCESS CATTER, LORD OF PRAY, QUEEN BEE, AND MIGHTY KING COCKROACH! ALL SPECIES WELCOME.

I wasn't in Europe.

I was at a Vegas sci-fi convention full of costumed weirdoes.

I raised a green arm, wiggled my legs in the short revealing tube dress, and gripped my face. Not that I could feel it, because it was covered in what I could only guess was hideous, prosthetic CATERPILLAR makeup.

Finally, the scream came, and when it did, the hundreds of frenzied fans lined up outside the ballroom noticed me and cheered.

"Princess! Our princess has arrived!"

"Scene stealer," Lord of Pray sighed. "Come on. Let's get you inside the ballroom."

Oh, I could just see Meredith up in her little bubble having a giggle. Let's "accidentally" stop in what appears to be lovely Italy but is really The Venetian, an Italian-themed Las Vegas hotel and casino with an upscale shopping center covered with a cloud-painted ceiling. The elaborate hallways, the singing gondolier, the massive ballroom—everything was designed to replicate Venice. Of course I'd bought it.

Meredith had not only baited me with the royal ball lie,

but had waited until my hopes were piqued to slap me into a Lycra caterpillar costume, showing off my larvalicious curves to fans who'd come to Vegas for a weekend devoted to their favorite sci-fi franchise, Mutant Insect Battalion.

Kind of tacky, Meredith said. I could hit her.

Lord of Pray led me over to the celebrity autograph table. Everyone snapped pictures paparazzi-like, although I doubted my photo would land on the cover of *Young Royals* magazine any time soon. According to the posters, I was just a cable actress named Mindy Myerson.

The shock of where I was and what I was doing did not die down over the next five hours of signing Princess Catter's name. Luckily, Mindy's life-size cutout was already auto-graphed, so I had a model. Anytime I accidentally began writing Desi, I'd switch it to "dear" or "desperately yours."

I mean, the job itself wasn't too awful—it still beat Pets Charming—but it was a pretty big letdown that Meredith had duped me into standing in for a C-list actress with her Great Princess Scam, which I so totally believed.

I did get to meet insects of all ages and sizes who'd flown in (not literally) from around the world for the convention. A shy, wispy girl around my age in a BUG OFF! shirt told me my hesitancy to enter my pupa stage made her feel better about her school life, which was weirdly flattering even though I had no clue what she meant. Some experiences were less heartwarming, like when a six-foot wood louse approached me with a poster-size collage of Mindy's pictures.

"I love you," he said.

"Er . . ." Uh-oh. I glanced around to see if someone nearby could help, like this supposed hidden sub Meredith had planted. "Thanks. You want me to sign something for you?"

"No, I want you to be my insect bride."

"Um, that's sweet, but roly-polys aren't really my type."

I spotted a woman in a bee costume pointing me out to a security guard, who readjusted his belt and began making his way across the room. The bee gave me a thumbs-up and slipped back into the crowd. Ah. Thank you, sub assistant!

The wood louse kneeled down—no easy feat in a foam costume—and pulled out an emerald ring. "Your betrothal to Lord of Pray is a flimsy charade. A bug like you deserves someone with a firmer exoskeleton."

Whoa. Fandom is one thing. Believing you're a wood louse with an actual exoskeleton is quite another. "Look, I'm not . . . It's a just a show. This isn't real."

"But my love for you is."

The security guard appeared with three others guards in tow. "Okay, let's go, buddy."

"True love stretches across classification systems!"

They dragged him away as a soothing voice filled the ballroom. "The ceremony will begin in five minutes."

Lord of Pray looped his third arm through mine and led me around the limitless rows of retail booths hawking comic books and action figures and more life-size cardboard cutouts of yours truly. I started to count off all the ways I'd been cheated. No princess dress. Instead of a romance with a prince, I got a proposal from a six-legged arthropod. I STILL hadn't escaped costume heads. And my chances of royal glamour on this job were as likely as that wood louse linking up with Mindy.

We reached the front of the ballroom. The stage was empty except for a closet-size box shaped like the end of a Q-tip.

"Okay, Mindy," Lord of Pray said. "Hop on to the stage—your wardrobe change is all ready. Get dressed and we'll set up the cables. Go flit around, and in an hour you and I will hit up the shops. You ready?"

Wardrobe change. And that was supposed to happen where, exactly? It would have taken hours to get Mindy into her current getup.

"Fellow arthropods!" The announcer waited for the cheering to die down. "Today we will witness the long-awaited transformation of Princess Catter into a pupa. Behold!"

A spotlight swallowed me in light. Lord of Pray nudged me onto the stage. I tugged on my dress, waiting for a cue.

One boy—his shaved head painted with extra eyes—called out: "To the chrysalis, Princess!"

The swelling crowd picked up the chant. "Chrysalis! Chrysalis!"

I reached my arms out. What should I do? Magically poof into a butterfly? Pull out a can of Raid and end this disaster?

The chanting died down and a heckler yelled, "Pupa yourself, already!"

Pupa yourself. Hmm. Now *that* would make a great T-shirt design.

Lord of Pray nodded toward the Q-tip thingy onstage. A door popped open.

"That's the chrysalis?" I whispered.

Suddenly, the stalker wood louse broke past a security guard and barreled onto the stage, a large mosquito net in his hands. "Don't pupa! I love you just the way you are!"

Holy wood louse. Chrysalis or not, I had to get away from my roly-poly Romeo. I dodged around him, the crowd egging me on, and jumped through the open-doored chrysalis, which was really a changing room with a blue butterfly costume laid out on a stool.

I peeled off the caterpillar face, dropping it onto the floor. If I hadn't been so bummed about the situation, I would have enjoyed the irony of it all. I was standing in the ultimate symbol of personal transformation. In a way, I was getting exactly what I wanted—a chance to change into something prettier, freer, with bigger possibilities. Now thousands of fans and an entire insect nation were counting on me to do just that. As fast as possible. I was halfway out of my dress when Meredith cleared her throat behind me.

"Was it a royal dream come true?" She snorted. For someone with such a raspy voice, her laugh was surprisingly piglike.

I covered my chest with the butterfly wings. "Meredith! I . . . you . . . I can't—"

"Relax, modest goddess. You're done. I've already

timed the rouge to deactivate in a minute or two—much easier to undo the façade than create it. You might not even notice. Usually we coordinate the sub's appearance to match their departing ensemble, but no need here, what with the costume change. So Mindy is ready to pop back in. She hates the caterpillar meet-the-fans part, but couldn't wait to butterfly above the crowd. I can't say I blame her. You looked ridiculous in the makeup."

She pointed her remote control at the stool, and our bubble oozed out, somehow fitting into the makeshift chrysalis.

I patted my stomach—all remnants of insect wear now gone, replaced by my FLOCCINAUCINIHILIPILIFICATION T-shirt. And I hadn't felt the change.

We eased into the bubble right as the announcer called, "Behold, Princess Flutter!"

"That was the stupidest thing I've ever done in my life," I said once we were safely in Meredith's office.

"Really?" Meredith swallowed another laugh. "You didn't like the fishnets?"

"No." I rolled my lips over my braces. "I didn't. And I seriously don't appreciate you telling me I'd be on royal duty when that was more like my Pets Charming job. I trusted you."

Meredith's smile vanished. "You think I'm going to drop you into some country without even knowing if you can hack it? No way. There's a limited number of royals left in the world, and we save our real subs for them."

"Well, I thought this agency was some big secret. Can't be too secret if you're letting actresses in on it."

"They're not *in* on anything. Mindy contacted us through the temp section of our agency. We use it to fill in for a few select beauty queens, actors . . . those sort. Really, it's just a cover for us to screen subs without exposing our secret. Mindy thinks you're just a dead-on look-alike in elaborate makeup and prosthetics, with a genius for fast getaways. She knows nothing about the rouge or MP or this bubble. So they get their temps—we get our tests."

"Still, you could have told me all that beforehand."

"And miss out on the fun? No way. Look, I don't know why this upsets you. Surprisingly, you passed." She twirled her finger around. "Whoop-dee-do for you."

"It was a big whoop-dee-do, thanks." I rubbed the back of my neck. "So the next job will be actual royalty, right? Something a little more glamorous?"

"I don't know about that. Princesses are people. Glamour is all relative."

"Hey, I've seen *Roman Holiday*. I don't buy into the woe-is-me princess stuff. It's still better than Pets Charming."

Meredith raised an eyebrow. "Well, since you're such an expert already, and you obviously don't need my far-more educated take, you can go lie down. It's good to decompress for a bit between jobs, clear your head. I'll slow down the bubble speed so I can get some work done, and you can sleep. You never know when you'll get a break around here."

My hand ached from the autograph blitz. I closed my

eyes and melted into the couch, forcing out all thoughts of insects. The whirring bubble and the never-ending tapping of the keyboard gradually lulled me into a peaceful sleep.

Peaceful, until the earthquake hit.

Chapter
7

"*E*arthquake!" I dove under the couch. The candies on the coffee table jiggled while the rest of the room jangled. The room sounded like it was in the middle of a washing machine during spin cycle. Oblivious, Meredith kept typing.

"Mer-e-dith. What's go-ing on?" I asked from under the protection of her furniture.

Meredith glanced up from her work. "What do you mean?"

"That shak-ing."

"Oh. That's turbulence. Only a few more minutes of this and then we land."

"Min-utes!" My eyes crossed and my teeth chattered. I was a coin stuck in the washer, spinning and spinning forever.

Just when I thought my bones would crack, the motion stopped. Meredith calmly stood up and exited the bubble. I followed, stumbling out like I'd gotten off a roller coaster. Three different Merediths swirled around me until they blended into one very impatient version.

"See? We're here. You're such a drama queen sometimes."

"Here" was an empty underground parking garage. The bubble floated in a "Reserved for M. Pouffinski" parking spot until Meredith hit a button and sucked it back into her remote.

She led me up a ramp, out of the parking lot, and onto the wet city street. Across from us, chic customers sipped coffee at an outdoor café under an overcast sky. Smooth, white, stone buildings with wrought-iron balconies and blue roofs lined the street. A modern, rectangular building tore into the skyline.

I gasped. "Meredith, are we in—"

"Paris, of course," she said without slowing down.

"Oh my gosh." Audrey Hepburn once said *Paris is always a good idea*, and here we were! For real. "So that Eiffel Tower over there"—I pointed to the structure in the far-off distance—"is the *real* Eiffel Tower, not a Vegas rip-off?"

A man on a scooter zipped past us and yelled something in French. "You wish," Meredith muttered.

"What did he—"

"Not something I intend to repeat. Hurry up."

A moment later we walked into the sleek, posh lobby of

a solitary black skyscraper, the Tour Montparnasse. Meredith flashed a sparkly green ID badge at a burly security guard, and led me into an elevator. "I'm Henry the Eighth I Am" played softly in the background.

"Didn't know they had a Muzak version of that one," Meredith mused as she shoved her card into a special slot, switching the light from red to green. At the top floor, the elevator stopped with a ding, and the doors scrolled open.

"I don't think we're in Idaho anymore, Toto," I whispered.

If you took the coolness of every fashion magazine in the world and mixed it in one sweet bowl of awesome, it would still be only one-tenth as amazing as this. The whole layout was über modern: geometrical furniture, odd sculptures, and thin vases filled with lilies. A stunningly beautiful receptionist sat at a round glass desk bearing the sign MIRAGE, AGENCE MODELESE. Behind her, elegant women in designer clothes flitted in and out of offices. Truly, Celeste Juniper would look like a clumsy hick next to the skinny gorgeous girls lounging on the white couches. So you can imagine how I felt standing in the middle of a Paris modeling agency in my FLOCCINAUCINIHILIPILIFICATION shirt and jeans. *Trés* vapor.

The receptionist didn't look up when we approached.

Meredith cleared her throat. "*Bonjour*. I need to—"

The girl pointed a perfectly manicured finger at the couches and spoke in a high, French-accented voice. "Vittorio is running late. Take a seat."

"No, no." Meredith slapped her green ID onto the counter. The girl glanced at it, then up at Meredith, her eyes widening. "Ms. Pouffinski, I'm so sorry. I'm new . . . I didn't realize you were an . . . an agent—"

Meredith laughed. "Did you think Desi here was a model?" I turned to glower at her, but then she added, "Don't you recognize new *talent* when you see it?"

The room hushed as if that word—*talent*—had magical freezing powers. A few models whispered to each other in French. I avoided the stares by focusing on a white, blobby sculpture.

"Desi will begin work immediately," Meredith said, "and she'll need a building ID badge with special access. At your convenience, of course."

"Of course," the receptionist said reverently.

Meredith rolled her eyes and started walking toward an empty hallway. "Desi, *vámonos*."

I scurried behind her, grateful to escape the stares of the beautiful people.

"What was that all about?"

"Mirage? That's our cover. On paper, Façade is technically a branch of Mirage. They don't have a clue what we do, but they worship us. As they should."

"Why did they act so shocked when you said I was a, um, talent?"

"It's rare and mysterious to them. A new talent doesn't walk in every day, so you're kind of a big deal. But whatever. Don't let it go to your head. You have work to do."

The last couple of things I mentally filed in the Meredith's rude comments folder, and I focused instead on the "You're kind of a big deal" part. As in, not vapor. As in, unique. As in, there were models sitting in that lobby who were envious of me because of my magical abilities.

Surreal much?

We stopped at a large door, where Meredith swiped her card again and positioned herself in front of a built-in computer screen. A red laser scanned up and down her features.

"Entry granted," said a computerized female voice.

And then the door clicked open, revealing the *real* reception area. And . . . wow.

I'd never been in a fairy-tale castle, but I imagined it must look something like this. Tall stained-glass windows cast a rainbow of sunshine on the gold-inlay floors. The cathedral ceiling was covered in silver stars carved into a midnight sky. A monstrous chandelier reached down, radiating a warm glow on the front reception area. The whole place exuded majesty. Centuries of it.

"But . . . it's a tower! The building was boxy and all glass. You couldn't even fit this room on the whole floor—"

"Desi. I have magic powder that morphs your physical appearance. I travel in a bubble. And you might not have noticed, but my hair is consistently fabulous. There are few limits to what we can do."

I heard a cough, then noticed a balding gentleman, more butler than receptionist, standing partly hidden behind a colossal bouquet of yellow roses.

"Ms. Pouffinski. Pleasure."

Meredith glowed. "Ferdinand! We're just on our way to substitute orientation. This is Miss Desi Bascomb."

"Ah, the new talent?" He gave me a small bow. "Lilith is expecting you. Genevieve was suddenly called away, but she sends a warm welcome."

Meredith seemed to deflate a little, but then she smiled. "Thank you. Desi?"

I waved at Ferdinand and followed Meredith down an echoey hallway lined with priceless-looking artifacts—fans, figurines, and silver trinkets, all with little engraved placards mounted below them. I paused at a tall white wig in a glass box and read the inscription: *To a true professional. Merci for saving my neck. Au revoir, Marie.* Like, Marie Antoinette? The French queen who was beheaded?

As if reading my mind, Meredith tsked. "History depends on who is writing it. Now check this out."

She pulled a golden curtain tassel to the right, unveiling a built-in display case filled with tiaras. I stood until my nose was inches away from the glass, gasping after reading the note attached to an emerald tiara. *You're a match made in heaven, Genevieve. XO, Princess Grace.* Oh my gosh. Princess Grace. Grace Kelly *wore* that.

"How do I get one?" I tapped the glass. "That is so cool!"

"Dream on, darling. They don't toss these things around. In fact, receiving a tiara from a client is an extremely rare honor. Let's move on. And try not to gape. It's unflattering."

I had to be a foot taller than Meredith, yet she stayed a

few steps ahead of me as we left the corridor and entered a more businesslike hallway that resembled a fancy law office. We even passed a row of seven silver-framed portraits. A somber bunch, all posing in the same velvet-backed chair, wearing the same superior frown. Yet everyone had crazy, colored hair like Meredith's. The woman in the center portrait actually had a rainbow hairdo. What was up with the bad dye jobs here? I'd have to ask later.

Meredith stopped in front of a purple door and waited for me to join her. Even then she didn't knock, but seemed frozen. "Lilith and some of the others are very traditional. I should be training you, but . . . it's complicated. Anyway, one of my subs accidentally got stuck in Siberia a few days ago, and I've got to go deal with that mess."

"Uh, what mess?"

"Oh." Meredith coughed. "We just haven't found her yet."

My eyes widened.

Meredith rolled hers. "It's been on my things-to-do list, okay?"

Finally she rapped the heart-shaped knocker three times. "I can do this," she whispered to herself before squeezing a smirk onto her face.

The door whipped open, revealing a stunning woman with a serene smile and cascading lavender hair that looked like she'd stolen it from a My Little Pony doll. "Oh, Meredith, sweetheart. I'm so glad you're here." Lilith's accent was . . . I couldn't place it . . . the accent of a girl who knows Latin, plays croquet, and goes to boarding school. Meredith's name sounded like music when Lilith said it. They air-kissed each other, and Lilith turned her serenity on me. "And you must be Desi. I'm Lilith. We are so insanely excited to have you!"

I grinned. "Thanks. Insane is a good word for all of this."

"I bet. Oooh, I want that T-shirt! So ironic. Where'd you get it?"

"I made it."

"A designer." She winked. "I'm loving you already. We were just finalizing the surrogate assignments for the Lady Carol wedding. Why don't you come in and I'll show off our new star!"

"I'll leave Desi for you, then—"

"Oh, don't be shy, Meredith." Lilith giggled. "Might be fun for you to see how we work at this level."

She swept us into a large conference room, brightly lit, with comfortable chairs, a long table, and a projection screen filled with notes and pictures of various royals. Framed maps hung on the walls. Women of different nationalities (and very different hair colors) sipped coffee or flipped through documents. Lilith clapped her hands. "Everybody! I want you to meet Desi, our new surrogate! Come welcome her before I sweep her off for her Level One training."

The group smiled at me warmly. Two women rushed over and gave me hugs. "Welcome to the Façade family! You are so lucky to have Lilith training you. She's just the best!"

Meredith stifled a yawn. "Yes, Desi is in for a *rare* treat. Would love to visit, girls, but if I don't go look after my clients, no one will."

A woman with pink hair smiled. "Oh, Meredith, don't rush off. Who *isn't* busy? Stay for a bit."

"Yes. A very little bit," added a lemon-haired agent.

"I know. It's been so long since we had girl time." Lilith wrapped her arm around Meredith's shoulder. Meredith looked like she was ready to heave. "You never told me if you found that poor sub who got lost. I can only imagine how awful that must have been."

"Right. Well, sorry, girls. Duty calls." Meredith turned her back to the other women. "Desi, I'll be back in a few hours with your first assignment. Just have to finalize the details, but I can tell you"—she raised her voice so the others could hear—"it's a big one. Ta-ta, girls!" With a neat pivot, Meredith left the break room.

"Charming as ever," Pink Hair said under her breath. "My name is Agatha, by the way."

"And I'm Priscilla," said Yellow Hair. "Now, tell us. What's Desi short for?"

"Nothing. Just Desi. It doesn't mean anything."

"Oh, I don't take much stock in name meanings." Lilith brushed her hand through her violet mane. "Mine has something to do with darkness. Ridiculous, right? That's what's so fun about being a surrogate. You get a new name for a while. And a new . . . everything."

The other agents laughed.

Their hair was just so bright. I had to ask. "You all have such colorful hair. I mean, it's pretty, but—"

"But?" teased Priscilla. "Don't you think we're fabulous?"

"Poor Desi, your head must be whirling," Lilith said, laughing. "You change your hair when you become an agent; it's a status mark of sorts. There's only a handful of us, and we were all once surrogates like you, you know, which meant we weren't allowed to see or interact with each other until we made our career move and ditched our *regular lives*."

"Not to mention the commute!" added Agatha.

"And trying to balance home life with work stuff." Priscilla shuddered. "Now we have an agency family."

So what was Meredith, then, the annoying stepsister? "That's cool," I said. "Doesn't the hair make people curious, though?"

"Oh, people lacking MP can't see it, Desi dear," Lilith said. "I'm a total redhead as far as they're concerned. And we don't spend much time out there in the normal world anyway, what with our busy schedules. Speaking of, I should steal you away for training."

Agatha smoothed down her blouse. "Yes, I think we're done here. I'll secure Emily for Princess Rachel, then. She's our strongest conversationalist."

"Just make sure she doesn't go *near* Rachel's history with the groom." Priscilla shook her head. "Ack, this wouldn't be so difficult if everyone wasn't skipping out. Lady Carol is such a beast; everyone wants a sub!"

"I bet her fiancé wants one too!" Agatha glanced back

at the screen. "We'll hammer it out. Go ahead, Lilith. And it was lovely meeting you, Desi."

"You too. I had no idea how . . . wonderful you'd all be."

Lilith wove her fingers into mine. "That's just because you're stuck with Meredith. She's not the warmest cookie in the batch." She squeezed my hand. "But we all know how special you are. Ready to get started?"

I looked down at our hands. Had Meredith even touched me, let alone shown warmth or kindness? No, all she'd done was roll her eyes and laugh at me. Oh, and pinch me.

And then there was Lilith.

"Yeah." I squeezed her hand back. "Princess me up."

Chapter 8

Lilith guided me into the classroom, a perfect mix of the modern outer reception area and the royal charm of the tower. One worn, heavy desk that had probably belonged to a little princess a few hundred years ago faced a glass-and-metal table with a swivel chair. An oriental rug covered the floor, and track lighting poked out from the ceiling. There was a "Subs Learn and Earn!" poster, and Lilith's desk held a few golden-framed pictures of her in different designer gowns.

"Let's go over our history first to give you an educated foundation." Lilith pointed a purple-jeweled remote at a blank screen that covered one entire wall, while I slid into my seat. "This first item is more precious to us than all those tiaras out there combined."

I expected to see a fat set of crown jewels, or maybe even a throne made out of diamonds. Instead, a picture of a small and very old turquoise statue filled the screen—something you might pass by in a museum on the way to the mummy exhibit.

"Is that a . . . is that a hippopotamus?"

"Yes. Hippopotamuses are very important in Egyptian history, and in Façade's as well. You see, this agency's beginnings trace back to an ancient Egyptian priestess, Woserit, who was the first to discover the magic of transformation." Lilith clicked to the next slide, a beautiful ebony statue of a woman's head. "There she is. Now, those were dark times. The royal court was buzzing with rumors of a plot to murder the queen. Woserit was by the Nile, pondering her queen's dire situation, when a hippo appeared and told her to rub some Nile silt onto her face—that's the active ingredient in the rouge, you know. The silt temporarily transformed her into the queen's double and inspired Woserit's plan: until the traitors were apprehended, the queen would hide, and Woserit would masquerade as the queen. That very night, the traitors poisoned her food, and Woserit died protecting the queen, thus sealing the magic to all who serve royalty."

"Wow," I said. "Didn't learn that in my sixth-grade Egyptian unit."

Lilith laughed and turned off the projector. The lights came back on. "Don't worry. We won't let you get killed. Any other questions?"

Uh, *yeah*. "How many subs are there?" I asked.

"Surrogates, dear. Call them surrogates. *Sub* sounds so common. Anyway, there are several fine surrogates employed by the agency. I would say there's about one surrogate for every six royals."

One for every six? So I guess I kind of *was* a big deal. And I probably had a good shot at subbing, er, surrogating for big-time royals! "One more. How do the levels work?"

"Levels are assigned to royals based on the their country's wealth, their world influence, the amount of protocol associated with the royal's title. . . . It's a very complex formula. Oh, and media attention." Lilith beamed and showed me her diamond bracelet. "This was a gift for a particularly tricky maneuver."

Tiaras, diamond bracelets. The job perks sure beat free Mountain Dew at Pets Charming.

"The higher the level," Lilith continued, "the more the client can expect from her surrogates—such as a mastery in all the basics: riding, literature, world history, art history, and classical music. It's a rare and talented individual who progresses past the first two levels. Only a select few ever match."

"Match?"

"Oh, Desi, it's the best. Matching is a surrogate's main goal. Once you've worked for a princess multiple times, you may apply to be her match—her permanent substitute. You get to grow with your client, become close to her family, and really *live her life*. You can see why it's important to be so keenly trained, right?"

"Yes. That's . . . there's so much involved," I said, feeling daunted.

"Well, royal life is culture at its highest. But don't worry, Desi dear, although it certainly doesn't help your case that you are working with Meredith. Don't get me wrong: she's talented, just a bit of a renegade. She used to be something of a protégé, but then there was that scandal."

I leaned in. "Scandal?"

Lilith waved her hand. "Oh, no. I did *not* mean to mention that. Let's just say it was enough to strain important professional relationships and revoke her training privileges, which is why I'm so lucky to be working with you now! You see, and this is just between us girls, I usually get the high-profile, elite jobs. Sometimes, if I see enough promise, I might take a Level Two. So keep that in mind after your Level One performance review. Surely you can do dressage, yes?"

Thanks for nothing, Cunningham Stables. "No."

"Any instruments? Archery? French literature?"

"I like theater," I said, feeling myself vaporize.

"Well, acting is the most important skill," Lilith said kindly. "But don't worry, we'll catch you up. Girls with MP are naturally fast learners. And far more mature than other girls. Besides, Level One really is the ideal practice turf because no one pays attention to those far-flung new royals and ugly ducklings. Now, I'll bring out the tea set. It's time to get down to business."

Back in Idaho I'd sat through ten months of Mom's charm

school wondering *When am I ever going to use this?* Well, question answered. With my mom it was all about local beauty pageants, and with Lilith it was about having tea with the Crown Princess of Japan. Lilith walked me through dinner and tea etiquette and the specific protocols that varied by culture and order of eminence—like, if you're a princess at a state dinner, no one may eat before you've tasted the food. Dream come true, right?

"That was fun, wasn't it? Let's move on to impersonation. My favorite." Lilith cleared away our delicious tea (I remembered not to slurp, but got a pinched look when I inhaled a pastry). She perched herself on the edge of my desk.

"Now, a good sub is like a Method actor. Here, let's try one role. Now, pretend you're Princess Desiree, a girl with a wild-child rep, and I am your haughty great-aunt Lady Lily. We're at a . . . let's say a new exhibit at the Louvre. Here we go." Lilith blinked and smiled a cool, perfectly royal smile. How did she do that? I swear her features all but morphed into a nosy aunt's. "So, Desiree, sweetheart! You look divine. How are things at school?"

"I . . . I, uh . . . Wait, I'm the princess right now, right?"

Lilith nodded demurely. "Do you need a moment to get into character?"

"Oh! Of course, sorry." I bit my lip and thought hard about this imaginary Desiree. Would a bad girl give her aunt snark? No, this might be the aunt who gives her the good presents. Better to ease into it. "School is, well, busy," I said, attempting a wild-child smile.

"Wonderful!" Lilith cooed. "Oh, Desiree, I worry about you so. How are your classes, dear?"

"They're . . . challenging. I really love art history, especially the Impressionists—"

Lilith rapped a ruler on the desk. "Oh, Desi. No no no. I understand, of course, your motives, but hon. You have no idea if this girl knows a Picasso from a Pissarro."

"But they *are* at an art museum. And her classes must be hard."

"Hmm. You're on the right track, but to be safe, you should never be so direct. What if I say, 'Oh? What do you think of Clement Greenberg's stance on modernism?'"

Clement who? "Uh . . ."

"See, you're stuck. Now, when you get in a bind like that, strategies include: coughing until someone offers you a beverage, changing the subject, or my specialty, flashing a royal jewel that somebody is bound to compliment. Worst-case scenario: fake laryngitis. Now, let's give this another try." With one blink, she flashed back into character. "So tell me, dear, how are your classes?"

This was tough. What if I didn't answer the question at all? "Well, you know how it is. Same old. I get so tired of *learning* sometimes."

Lilith patted my hand as if to say good job, but stayed right in character. "What's this I hear about Duke Wellingford's daughter and the dog walker? Poor thing, she must have no self-esteem because of her looks. A dog walker! Can you believe it?" Lilith sniffed.

"Maybe she really loves him?" I said, uncomfortable with Lilith/Lily's tone. "I hope she's doing all right."

"Desi, Desi," Lilith sighed. "If a royal gets caught with a dog walker, she's totally free game. Plus, gossip is an excellent way to bond with another royal, not to mention a vastly entertaining pastime."

I noticed I'd twisted the hem of my T-shirt into a knot. "But what if I think it's mean? What if I want to stop Lady Lily from trashing someone who might be really struggling?"

"Method, Desi. You become that princess in your head, and you ONLY do as the princess would do. It's so much fun that way!" She punctuated her words with her hand, like she was painting the image for me in the air. "Think of it. When you surrogate for a bratty princess, you get to BE bratty. When I was a surrogate, now and then I'd send my food back even if it was perfectly fine. Just because I *could*."

Yeah, but weren't they ever tempted to see what other uses there were for this magic? Look at the situation—I could help change Lily's snobby opinion of the dog walker. Help this poor girl out!

Just because, you know, I *could*.

"Oh, dear. Look at the time!" Lilith exclaimed after we'd been practicing our impersonations for what felt like hours. As different princesses, I'd attended a funeral, presented an award, and posed for a photo shoot. "We have a few minutes. Why don't we go check out Central Command?"

I followed Lilith into the hallway, feeling like my feet

75

weren't quite touching the floor. That vaporiness I often felt at home was evaporating fast, almost to the point of a massive happy explosion.

"Now, Central Command, or CC, is where the tech people work," Lilith told me. "You know, monitoring bubble flight paths, rouge algorithms, Princess Progress Reports, things like that. Ooh, and you still need to get your manual!"

Before I could ask what these things were, we came to the wall of portraits. "That's the CEO or something, right? What's her name again?" I pointed at Rainbow Hair.

"Genevieve? Oh, I could write a whole book about Genevieve's brilliance. She's the head of the Façade council, and I feel like she's my personal mentor. When the PPRs are uploaded to our network by the princesses, Genevieve is the one who reviews them for the Court of Appeals. She also monitors all the agents and decides which princesses qualify for our services. She knows everyone who's anyone and knows all their business. Their private business. If you look at it a certain way, you could say she's the most powerful woman in the world."

What I saw next seemed to confirm Genevieve's power. In three steps we went from Camelot to Façade's version of Mission Control. Ten casually dressed, surprisingly young employees, each sitting at a large round table, wheeled their chairs from one computer to another, frantically typing and checking the large screen in the front of the room. Graphs and diagrams and numbers flashed on the screen above a large world map with unlit red lights sprinkled across it.

"Who are these guys?" I asked.

"These are people with MP whose special talents are more . . . technological. I have no idea how we recruit them; they aren't terribly exceptional. Not like surrogates or agents."

On the world map, a light in eastern China blinked for a second, and everyone stopped what they were doing to stare. They let out a sigh when it didn't stay lit.

"MP meter," Lilith whispered. "You should have seen Meredith's face when they picked up on your signal. The strongest one we'd had in a year."

"Really?"

"Indeed. Now, let's get you your new toy!"

Lilith led me to an adjacent room, where a cute high school–age guy in a rocker T-shirt and worn Converse was sitting at a desk covered with laptops and crusty coffee mugs. Lilith coughed, and the boy looked up.

"What can I do for you, Lilith?" he said. "And who's your friend?" He smiled at me, and I felt my face flush.

"Hank, meet Desi Bascomb, our newest surrogate. We came to pick up Desi's manual."

"Oh, right." He ran over to another desk and rummaged through a tower of tangled cords and spare parts. "Sorry for the mess. Things have been pretty hectic. We finished installing that new PPR interface and found out some of the multimedia components aren't compatible with the Princessnet security shield."

Lilith raised an eyebrow. "What does that mean in English?"

"Ah well, there's a programming glitch. When the PPRs come in, the network computers go haywire and start levitating." Hank smiled when my eyes widened. "Magic and technology follow different rules, so they're bound to butt heads sometimes. Right now the levitation is totally getting in the way of our monitoring system."

"So no Princess Progress Reports are coming through?" Lilith asked, alarmed.

"Just for a bit! No worries. Ah, here we go." He held up a silver touch-screen computer/phone that he carefully placed into my hands.

"Seriously, don't drop, shake, break, or lose this. This is an exquisite piece of technomagical machinery, and it's worth some serious dough." He scratched his chin. "Well, I've got to figure this PPR thing out before the Lady Carol wedding, so uh . . . glad to have you on board, Desi. Peace out."

We returned to the loud chaos of CC. Meredith was standing in the doorway, her eyes scanning the room.

Lilith enveloped me into a hug and whispered, "Last thing. Meredith may seem hard on the outside, but she's actually rather soft. Well, her ideas are soft. Limiting. Too . . . *of the people* for my tastes. So don't listen to her. Use your training. If you can make it through her boring gigs, we'll make sure Level Two is completely A-list, all right?"

I pulled away. "Yeah. Thanks."

Meredith marched over. "Where have you been? I've been looking everywhere."

Lilith gave me a tiny wink. "Just showing Desi around. She's such a quick study, we had some extra time."

Meredith looked skeptical. "Well, that's good news, because Desi's got an important assignment we need to get to. Let's go." She motioned for me to follow, and huffed away.

"Remember everything I taught you, Desi dear," Lilith said. Then she lowered her voice. "It might be the only help you get."

Chapter
9

Meredith waited for me in the hallway. "Training. Good?"

"Great! Lilith is—"

"Awful. I know. Sorry you had to deal with her."

"No, I think she's amazing. Really helped me out. Totally warm and—"

"Condescending?"

"Informative, actually," I said.

Meredith raised her chin. "Right. Opinions on that matter vary greatly, but some of us aren't as good at reading people as others."

I shrugged. As far as I was concerned, Lilith was easier to read than Gracie's flash cards, and so . . . *not* Meredith.

"Did you find your missing sub?" I asked.

"Yes, thank you, and I don't need your cheek," Meredith snapped. "Only a mild case of hypothermia. And thanks to her, you have a gig that's probably above your level." Meredith surveyed the empty hallway and opened the door next to Central Command. A broom closet. "Get in."

I followed her, wondering what level of crazy she had finally reached.

"Princess Simahya is Level One, but that's only because she's the youngest sibling and slightly . . . odd."

"Odd?"

She huffed. "Contrary to what Lilith may have taught you, odd royals are royals too."

"Meredith, I never said—"

"Now"—she cut me off—"since we're running late, I'm going to have to break protocol and launch from here. Don't tell. Just another outdated rule." Meredith pointed her phone into the darkest corner and leaked the bubble out. "Come on. You need to rouge up soon. And you can read about your first job while we fly."

Once we were safely in the air, Meredith gave me a quick tutorial on my manual and made me promise to guard it with my life and only read it in a safe, private place. The constant possibility of a Sub Spotting might have scared me if I hadn't been so pumped about the device itself. I had to get one of these for school!

The home screen was divided into sections that each had a cute icon. A sun for the weather, a compass for the

GPS system, a tiara for princess mail (with a message already there!). Some even had little captions underneath, like the lipstick for beauty and health tips (top energy bars for the sub on the go); a high heel for royal fashion (a crash course on the four C's of diamonds); a horse for royal skills (how to shoot an arrow without killing your princess); and best of all, a winking eye for gossip (scandals of Lady Jana: the lady-in-waiting who just can't wait).

I couldn't resist clicking on the winking eye first. Shots of various princesses splattered the page, organized by region. For each princess there was a message board where subs could anonymously post helpful nuggets. I read through a few:

> **Fturagent3**: Princess Jamelia says she's a vegetarian, but then what's with the McDonald's wrappers under her bed?

> **OrngNewPink**: Duchess Olivia is totally anal about her tan lines. Follow her tanning schedule exactly. Don't do what I did and try to cheat with self-tanner. Worst PPR *ever*.

> **SportySub**: Baroness Anne and the Duchess of Watershire are STILL not talking after the Poodle Incident. In fact, steer clear of all pooches. Things could get catty.

I did a search on Princess Simahya and came up with one comment:

> **AfricanPrincess**: She's really quiet and likes to eat. A LOT.

If you shut your mouth except when you're shoving food into it, you'll do fine.

What a mean thing to say! I considered posting this, but was too excited to read the message waiting in my inbox. I clicked on the e-mail and instantly the full details of my very first royal adventure filled the screen.

At the top was a photograph of the palace (yeah, PALACE), and I kid you not, half of Sproutville could have fit inside. Flamboyant gardens surrounded the compound, and loads of expensive cars lined the driveway.

In her profile picture, the princess was looking down, like she was scared of cameras. And if it hadn't been for the title above her name, you'd have thought she was just a regular, kind of pudgy teenager.

Next, she'd posted a family picture with all her siblings' names and ages captioned below. It was a beautiful picture of everyone but Simahya, who had her eyes closed and wasn't smiling. Even her father, middle-aged with a round stomach and bulbous nose, looked handsome in it. And too bad for Simahya, she looked nothing like her beautiful mother—but her older sister, Nabila, did.

Even her personal information read like she was trying to rush through it so she could go back to being unnoticeable.

Princess Simahya bint Zafir bin Sultan al-Dhayrif

(Everyone just calls me Simmy)

Age: 13

Hometown: Al Hayrah

Favorite Color: Orangish Reddish Yellow. Ish.

Favorite Book: *The Trumpet of the Swan* by E. B. White. Or any romance. Especially ones with strong women and shirtless men.

Favorite Food: (with pictures of three different dishes below it). Sweets. Also chicken with nuts in spicy marinade. And fresh-baked rosemary bread. Wait, do I have to pick one?

Family Background: My father is Sheikh Zafir. As sovereign prime minister, he oversees oil distribution for the entire western coast, so he's never around. My mother is also gone a lot—she's flying in from Europe just in time for the charity event. Queen Raelena is visiting! Plus, all of our aunts and uncles and cousins from both sides of the family are staying with us this week. Fifteen women and only twelve bathrooms. Yikes! I'm SO glad you're coming.

I have two brothers and a sister, Nabila, who thinks she's in charge of everything. Seriously, don't sneeze unless you have her permission. Actually, just avoid her if you can. Also avoid Mrs. Farahani, our family PR coordinator. She and Nabila are always telling me what to do. Wish I could tell them a thing or . . . Never mind. Follow their lead. Or not. Whatever.

Cultural Traditions: We're Muslim, so don't dress, um . . . provocative. Not that I could look provocative. And since I'm the youngest girl in the whole family, I have to show extra respect to everyone. (You'll see why I don't talk all that much.)

Anything Else We Should Know: What, like interests? I've played the French horn since I was little, but only in the privacy of my room. I'm maybe, well probably, well definitely good enough to play for others, but no one around here would want to hear it. And I love American soap operas. Oh, and ducks. I'm a big fan of ducks. Just check out my room.

The bubble bounced once or twice before skidding to a stop. I realized the jewel on my rouge compact had already turned green. My hands shook as I brushed on the powder.

"We're here?" I held up my manual. "This is all the info I get?"

Meredith looked up from her laptop. "What do you mean?"

"If I'm going to inhabit Simmy's character, I need more important info than horns and ducks. What about religious customs? And memories and inside jokes and all of that?"

"I'm so tired of that Method nonsense. Look." Meredith lowered her voice. "This wouldn't have been something that Lilith would mention, but you can also use your MP as a kind of . . . compass. It takes some finessing, of course. I've found my MP to have its own frequency. When my mind is wandering, I can't tune in. But when I focus on the princess's needs, I mean really focus, everything else shifts away and I can sense what the princess would feel. It's a very Zen experience. You just have to be careful to channel, not meddle. Besides"—she pointed at me with a green pen—"if Simmy thought you needed to know her entire history, she would have put it in there. Do you follow?"

"I guess so. But what if she was in a hurry?"

"You're going to be okay as long as you pay attention. You learn the most by listening and reading between the lines. And lucky for you, Simmy is quiet and awkward. Easy."

"Oh, er . . . thanks for the tips."

"All right. Well, off with you," Meredith said. "See you in a few days."

Days? Feeling light-headed, I slid out of the bubble and into a grand, mirrored hallway. The color scheme was totally King Midas—gold on gold on gold. On gold. The fragrance of exotic flowers overpowered me.

I hid in a shadowy alcove while the Royal Rouge took over. The strangest part was how *surface* the transformation felt. In addition to the itchiness, I felt an occasional tug or pull. For some reason my elbows itched the most. And I swore I heard the faintest buzzing as it happened, like an electric razor was shaving all the Desiness away from me.

When the sensation stopped, I stole a peek into one of the nearby mirrors and almost jumped back from my reflection. I touched my/her/our hair. Darker, coarser, longer. My waistline and thighs were more potato than string bean. Orange fabric bunched together in what I could only guess was a dress. I smiled at her. She smiled back. Her mouth was wide and braces-free. I wondered if that meant I could eat caramel. . . .

Just when I was ready to make a move, about two dozen women of various ages swept past me, laughing and chattering. Some wore scarves over their heads, and their wild tops and designer jeans were trendier than anything in Sproutville.

I was watching them hurry past when an older, skinnier version of Simmy grabbed my arm. *Nabila.* "Simmy, I need to talk to you about something," she whispered. My thighs squished together as she dragged me into a crowded sitting room and directed me to a corner in the back. She pushed two chairs secret-sharing close and leaned forward.

"It's your weight," she said matter-of-factly. "I don't know how you've managed it, but you've obviously gotten even bigger since your weigh-in last month. I'm saying this because you're my little sister and I'm looking out for you. I think it's best if you hang back during photo ops this week. Also, Mrs. Farahani and I have arranged a special diet for you starting tomorrow."

Diet! My stomach rumbled at the thought. So much for caramel.

Nabila's lips curved into a fake, sympathetic smile. "Our fitness says a lot about who we are as a family, Simmy. And with Queen Raelena here, we're really going to be in the spotlight. So stop eating and avoid the cameras. Can you handle that?"

"Um—"

"Good girl, Simmy." Nabila patted my hand. "You're welcome."

The sound of applause echoed throughout the room, and we turned to see a young, sharp-looking woman—Mrs. Farahani—wearing a red skirt-suit and an almost psychotically large smile. "Welcome, everyone! On behalf of His Royal Highness Sheikh Zafir bin Abrakan al-Dhayrif and his family, I extend heartfelt thanks to all of you for attending this momentous event. As you know, we are expecting a most esteemed guest, Queen Raelena, to our upcoming gala in support of education for underprivileged young women, through the Daughters of Hope charity."

Excited murmurs filled the room.

"Her Royal Highness is admired across the world not only for her beauty and eloquence, but for her unparalleled charitable efforts; she was so pleased with our own beloved Princess Nabila's work with Amnesty International, she referenced the princess in a recent *Dateline* interview, which has produced some positive press for our country."

At this, all the women applauded and turned to smile at Nabila, who was just eating it up.

Mrs. Farahani continued. "So it's no surprise that this weekend we'd like to continue our focus on strengthening our relationship with our neighboring countries and our reputation as a world leader in progressive initiatives. We're here to relax and mingle, and perhaps brainstorm other ways to shine in Queen Raelena's eyes. Ah, the food is here!"

The room once again filled with vibrant conversations as a staff of uniformed servers wove through the crowd bearing trays of delicious-looking hors d'oeuvres.

One by one, the women rushed over to praise Nabila. No one gave me so much as a glance. *What would Simmy do?* Well, she'd be hungry (uh, who wouldn't be after smelling those pastries?), and Nabila was busy being adored, so . . .

I reached for a puff pastry, and Nabila whirled around and slapped my hand. "Simmy! I can't believe you."

Believe *me?* It's one little pastry, lady. A *spinach* one. "But I'm hungry!"

"Excuse me, girls, I'll just be a second." Nabila grabbed my arm and dragged me over to Mrs. Farahani.

"Simmy is *hungry*," Nabila announced. "I already brought up the issue with her, but she apparently doesn't care about this family."

I squirmed out of Nabila's grip, fuming. This whole conversation was so unreal. Simmy was a PRINCESS, not some naughty kid stealing cookies from the cookie jar. Mmmm, cookies.

Mrs. Farahani gave me the once-over and a condescending smile. Great. Nabila part *deux*. "Princess Nabila tells me your body mass index is twenty-eight. Did you know that is considered overweight, Your Highness?"

I felt my—Simmy's—cheeks burn. "I, well—"

"Now, what kind of image does an overweight royal send to the world?"

"Image? I think it just means—"

"Self-indulgence, Your Highness," she said. "And I mean this with all respect, but we're trying to cultivate a reputation for tireless service to the community, not to your stomach."

Don't talk back. Don't talk back. "I need to go to the bathroom. I'll see you in a bit."

In sixth grade, after my social life turned disastrous, I developed a special skill for locating bathrooms; you never know when you're going to need a refuge. This bathroom was at least gold-free—airy and cool with a view of the sun setting over a breathtaking walled-in garden. I wondered if Simmy ever hid in here to cool down. I mean, was this what her LIFE was like? Man, I'd eat all day long just to spite these jerks. Size doesn't define worth, people!

As I shuffled back down the hallway, I heard Nabila's voice mingling with Mrs. Farahani's. I paused just outside the room.

"We'll have to get a stylist in to help your sister, pronto." Mrs. Farahani said. "She looks like an orange in that dress."

Oh, that's original. An orange orange. Way to branch out.

Nabila snorted. "Don't compare her to food. She'll eat herself."

You know what? The weight cracks? They hurt. They weren't even talking about ME, but it still hurt. It hurt like Celeste taking my head off, or Hayden ignoring me, or Kylee not understanding. And this was Simmy's *family* here. If you can't be yourself around them, then when are you ever your-self?

I cleared my throat and turned the corner, leaning on the domed entryway.

At least Mrs. Farahani blushed.

Nabila flipped her hair. "Oh, Simmy. How long have you been out there?"

"Long enough."

They grew silent, throwing knowing glances back and forth.

And somehow their smugness made everything clear. Meredith had said my MP could be a compass, and right now every zinging nerve pointed to the fact that Simmy needed someone to stand up for her or else this bullying would never end. Channeling, meddling, whatever . . . I could feel the rightness of it.

And, you know, back in Idaho I'd made that wish, thinking I wanted the glamour of Grace Kelly. But what made her so impactful went beyond glamour. I mean, Nabila was gorgeous and graceful, but *so* not Grace Kelly.

Really, no immortal screen siren would sit back and let this nonsense continue.

"Simmy, when you stare like that, it makes your eyes bulge," Nabila finally said.

Oh yes. I was going to impact this girl like a meteor hitting the earth.

I swallowed a nasty comment, figuring it best to strategize before striking. "I'm going to bed," I said in as calm a voice as I could manage before leaving the room and running down the hall.

When I was alone, I turned on the manual and browsed through the applications until I found the compass icon. A map of the palace's interior appeared with a little red dot marking my current location.

The palace was so huge that even with my handheld GPS system, it took me twenty minutes to find the door with a tacked-on sign—a watercolor of a duck with the words "Please stay out. Please?"

I pushed open the door. *Yowza.* Simmy wasn't kidding about the ducks. There were shelves and shelves of collectibles—ceramic ducks and rubber ducks and cartoon ducks and a duck piñata. A mobile of toy ducks flew in V formation above her bed. Even her sheets were covered with the little quackers.

On her nightstand sat a worn copy of E. B. White's *The Trumpet of the Swan*, next to an old tape player. I hit PLAY, and a sweet, clear horn filled the room. Just one horn with no backup instruments, but it sounded like a whole orchestra. When the tape ended, I clicked open the player and read, "Simmy French Horn Practice." She'd been beyond modest in the profile. The girl could *play*. I couldn't believe no one knew about her talent.

Exhausted, I found some pajamas and crawled into bed, thinking about how in every fairy tale, the heroine's problems melt away when she becomes a princess—everyone sees how special she is and loves her. None of the stories was about a chubby, lonely princess who played the French horn into a tape recorder in her duck-filled bedroom. Or about the chubby princess's substitute, for that matter.

Maybe that's what made them fairy tales.

Real life is never how you dreamed it.

Chapter
10

The next two days weren't easy. Nabila's diet plan consisted of a handful of dates and gallons of nasty tea that had me searching for the little princess's room every five minutes. And it was an absolute waste because the rouge made me look like Simmy, not *become* Simmy. She wouldn't lose the weight—I would.

Besides, crash dieting so obviously wasn't the way to go if Nabila really wanted to help Simmy long-term. The rouge didn't give me any sense of Simmy's health, but spending entire days on cardio machines couldn't be good for anyone. Only three clicks through the health section in the manual was all I needed to find and print out a beginner's workout routine, which I left on the treadmill in case Simmy wanted to use it.

Dates and tea. Give me a break.

The plus side—it made the impersonation thing total cake. (Mmmm, cake.) With all the excitement going on, no one ever joined me in the gym. Heck, I even looked up a back-to-school mini workout in the manual and did a few sets of squats while engrossed in a *Days of Our Lives* love triangle playing on the gym's TV.

The day of the banquet, I showered after a yoga workout and found a blush-pink gown Mrs. Farahani had laid out on my bed with the note, *Good work, Your Highness! See you in make-up. Respectfully yours, Mrs. Farahani.* Respectfully. Whatever.

Worse, the dress was too tight and made Simmy's stomach bulge. I had to share a makeup artist and hair stylist with two cousins, and they hogged the beauty team for so long that the stylists never got to me. Before Mrs. Farahani could rush us out, I managed to smear on a bit of eye shadow and pin up Simmy's thick hair. Her hair looked pretty up. I'd have to tell her that.

Gown swishing (and thighs squishing), I followed Mrs. Farahani to a back entrance of the gold room, where the royal family had formed a long receiving line. At the head of the line, Simmy's mom, stunning in a conservative plum gown, stood next to Simmy's dad, the squat but handsome sheikh. Then came Simmy's uncles, brothers, and boy cousins, followed by Nabila and the rest of the women. Guests had already begun to pour in—royals and dignitaries from different countries, dressed in every style of regalia.

Diamonds and emeralds sparkled everywhere.

"Smile, Simmy. You look petrified," Mrs. Farahani said, startling me. She ushered me to the end of the line, a safe distance away from the first guest. I used my wait time to force myself to stop shaking.

Luckily, by the time anyone made it all the way through the line, they'd breeze past me, probably thinking, *Only one more princess until we grub.* Which was helpful because, despite the rouge, there was still a language barrier. I only understood the languages Simmy spoke. She clearly knew a lot, because I was able to pick up most of what people said, but some of the accents were thick, and my dress was tight, and I was starving. I endured it all in one breathless haze.

And I thought junior high was harsh.

The line was beginning to trickle off when a bald man in a white tie bowed before me. He said a quick intro, and when he stepped to the side, I realized who was next in line.

Queen Raelena. I suppressed a gasp. I'd seen her on *Oprah.* Her beauty was even more pronounced in person, not to mention that she was one of the most admired royals, who took impact to the highest level. Seriously, it was probably the biggest moment of my life, having such an amazing woman smiling at me. My knees wobbled as I bowed low. "It is an honor to meet you, Your Majesty."

"Your Highness." Queen Raelena bowed, her chocolate curls dipping with her. When she was again standing, a large elephant brooch glinted on her green satin gown.

I didn't know if I should bow again, or grovel, or kiss

her perfect feet, or what. Lilith had said compliments worked. I started there. "I love your brooch," I said.

She rubbed her fingers along the silver trunk. "Thank you, Your Highness. I have quite a fondness for elephants."

"They're lovely animals," I agreed. All those people walking past had made me desperate for good conversation; plus, the queen was like the sun. I just wanted to bask in her warmth. "I like ducks. I mean, I collect them. Not real ducks, but . . . uh, figurines."

I swallowed. Something was in my throat. Perhaps it was my foot.

Queen Raelena's eyes twinkled. "Well then, this is a pleasure. What brings about this interest, Your Highness?"

"Simmy. You can call me Simmy." I racked my brain. *Why ducks?* Then I thought of the mobile above Simmy's bed. "Have you ever seen ducks fly in formation?"

She nodded, so I kept going.

"It's so amazing. I read once that when one of the ducks is weak or injured, the other ducks form around it and make sure that it doesn't fall behind." Okay, little stretch of Lilith's rules of impersonation, but this was for a great cause. I mean, ducks? How do you explain ducks? Besides, if there was one thing Simmy understood, it was the yearning to be included. "And that's like this fund-raiser, actually. We need to stick together to make sure every girl has a chance for an education. Sometimes I wish people were, well, more like that. So yeah, I'm pro . . . duck."

Queen Raelena clasped her hands around mine for a

moment. "That is wonderful to hear. These events"—she lowered her voice—"you start to wonder if the involvement is just for the show."

"Of course. I feel the same way. We have such an opportunity to make an impact."

"We need more royals with such perspective. I'm sure this passion will lead you down an excellent path. Do you have any other interests, Simmy?"

After all Simmy's bad treatment, it was beyond awesome to finally talk to someone interested in her. Not to mention Queen Raelena. I mean, holy ducklings! I was talking to Queen Raelena! "Music. I play the French horn." And hey, if I'm going to brag on the girl, might as well give it some punch. "I'm not in an orchestra, but I've done some performances, and the audience has always been extremely complimentary. I really enjoy it." No need to mention that the audience was a stuffed waterfowl collection that lacked the ability to voice an opinion. Er, quack one.

A man, possibly a bodyguard, stepped to the right of the queen and whispered, "It seems dinner service is beginning."

The receiving line deteriorated, leaving only the two of us standing near the entry hall while others searched for their seats.

"Well, Princess Simmy, I'd love to hear you play someday." She bowed again. "Lovely to meet you."

"Thanks so much for talking to me!" I said brightly. "Let's go eat. I'm famished."

* * *

Elegant round tables filled the banquet room, plus one long table at the front for the royal family. Sheikh Zafir sat in the middle, whispering to Mrs. Farahani while the sheikha sipped her water. I took my seat at the end and unfolded my napkin onto my lap, grateful Simmy wasn't known for chitchat. Although, it was pretty lame that her parents hadn't even talked to me yet. I wondered what they thought of Nabila's starvation diet.

The first course was brought out, mini-fruit sculptures cemented with cream, but the server walked right past me. Another followed and spooned smooshed yellow vegetables onto my plate that smelled faintly of garbage.

"Simmy," Nabila whispered across the table. "Don't eat too much of that."

I shoved a forkful of the foul veggies into my mouth and swallowed. It was the only way I could stop myself from screaming.

About fifteen minutes later, the sheikh gave a nod and the servants removed the food. As gross as the vegetable stuff was, it was all I'd eaten that day. I eyed the towering fruit centerpiece. If only.

The trend continued for the next seven courses. The more tantalizing everyone else's food, the more inedible my course was. Dates. Grainy bread. Bitter broth. I was about to point at something and grab an apple pastry, when the sheikh stood and everyone stopped talking.

"I would like to thank you all for joining us this evening, particularly since our family has not congregated for a public event in some time. But our central reason for being here is to raise funds for the Daughters of Hope charity. Before we begin the auction, however, I'd like to make a toast to the guest of honor this evening, Queen Raelena."

Sheikh Zafir listed some of the queen's amazing credentials—her charities, her programs, and her trips around the world to promote peace and speak out against injustice toward women. "And, of course, the international media continues to include her on the top of all the beautiful-royals lists, which I myself am still hoping to make." The crowd laughed. "I would offer more, but I fear we shall reach morning before her accomplishments are adequately expressed. Please join me in raising a glass to Queen Raelena."

We raised our glasses and drank. Mine was a pungent punch. Hello! Isn't water fat free?

I heard a little beep coming from my clutch. Ah, the rouge's timer! Simmy was on her way back. Which meant I could beg Meredith for some food in about half an hour. I was almost done. No big mistakes made!

The queen stood and bowed to Sheikh Zafir. "Thank you, Your Majesty. And thank you for the opportunity to visit your home and meet your family. I've been greatly moved by your hospitality."

Nabila beamed as if the compliment were directed at her.

"Earlier, I had the particular pleasure of getting to know Princess Simmy, who I find possesses the empathy we leaders need to develop if we really want to help women in need."

Nabila's mouth dropped open. I shrugged innocently.

"I have a feeling this unique young royal has a bright future ahead of her. And so, I'd like to start this auction off today with a bid for Princess Simmy. Five hundred thousand dirhams from my own foundation to the Daughters of Hope charity, if she will perform for us on her French horn."

The crowd burst into applause. The sheikh glanced at the sheikha, who gave a confused shrug. They turned their gaze on me. "I'm sure my daughter would be honored to play for us all," the sheikha said. "Nabila, go fetch your sister's instrument. Everyone enjoy some pudding as we wait."

The servers rushed in with trays of sorbet. Queen Raelena gave me a thumbs-up sign. I would have given her one back, but I was temporarily paralyzed.

An entire room of royals and rich people and rich royals were waiting for me to perform on an instrument I wasn't sure I'd even seen before. Mom said bragging leads to trouble, and man, was she right. One blow on that horn and this would undoubtedly go down in Façade history as the most-witnessed Sub Spotting of all time. Maybe they'd even cut off my head and add it to their agency trophies.

"Father," I said through a frozen smile.

He wiped some pudding off his mustache. "Is there a problem, Simahya?"

One little one. I'm not really Simahya, and I don't know how to play the French horn. "I'm sick. I can't perform."

"What do you have?"

I watched Queen Raelena greet someone with a bow. Her brooch glinted in the light. "Elephantitis. Yeah. Really, really mild case. Just affecting the fingers. Comes and goes. Caused by stress."

Sheikh Zafir laughed. "Funny. I can see why Queen Raelena was so charmed."

"Right. Totally joking about the elephantitis." Went a little big with that lie. How about . . . "What I meant to say is . . . I feel . . . faint. All this dieting has drained my energy."

The sheikha leaned across the table. "Dieting? What dieting?"

Mrs. Farahani cut me off before I could answer. "Nabila was worried about Simmy's health, Your Majesty, so we suggested she cut back a little on her food intake."

Cut back a little? When your MAIN course is a date, that's more than a little.

"That's very thoughtful." Sheikh Zafir scratched his chin. "Did a nutritionist set up this diet, then?"

"No," I said, feeling very calm and strong. Was this the sixth sense Meredith was talking about? "It's a total crash diet and I hate it. I've already started an exercise plan, and I want to choose my own diet, not just for one event, but to feel better. Period. Right now I'm starving and tired and don't know how I'll be able to play my horn."

The sheikh and sheikha exchanged glances, obviously unaware of my inedible dinner, just as they were probably unaware of most everything Simmy did. A server materialized out of nowhere with all the missed dinner courses.

"I hope this restores your energy," the sheikha said. "We'll talk to Nabila later. Now eat up. We look forward to your performance."

I started with the apple pastry and went into a three-minute fork frenzy. But by the time I'd eaten enough to tame my hunger-induced delirium, and remembered the whole reason I was faking the faint thing to begin with, Nabila was back. I swallowed the last bite. I was fresh out of ideas and still had a good ten minutes until Simmy returned.

"Here, Simmy." Nabila held out my horn with a limp wrist. What a bizarre instrument. Why'd it have to be so big? How did you blow in it? What were all those swirly things? Why couldn't Simmy have played the maracas?

My options were zilch. I reached out for it. "Thanks."

I'm sure what happened next wasn't an accident. French horns are heavy; they can't be casually tossed. But that's what Nabila did. I lunged to catch it, but it banged on the floor. The guests gasped.

I hoisted it up. The mouthpiece had been twisted into a sharp ninety degree angle. Evil Nabila. There was no way I could play this now that she'd . . .

Wait.

Bless you, petty, awful Nabila. I shall erect a shrine in your likeness at Façade. Nabila: the Demon Princess who tried to smash a dream and instead saved the day.

"The mouthpiece is bent. I can't play." To prove my

point, I blew a note. Well, what was intended to be a note. The guests grabbed their ears. None of them seemed to notice the bubble that also blew out of the horn. It blossomed to full size right in the middle of our table. Meredith popped her head through the side and mouthed the words "Simmy's room. Five minutes," before disappearing again.

Saved by the bubble.

Queen Raelena rushed over. Nabila covered her mouth in mock dismay and said, "Oh, I am so sorry! This is horrible. I mean, I could sing instead, if that would help. I have had classical—"

"I'm sure Your Highness is a fine performer, but the bid was made for Princess Simmy." Queen Raelena clasped her hands over her mouth as if she were praying, before lowering them to reveal a bemused smile. "Actually, perhaps we could hold an event in my country, and Princess Simmy may perform then?"

"Oh, we can come together! Simmy is so shy—"

"Actually, maybe I should go alone." I flashed Nabila my greatest that's-what-you-get-for-being-so-awful-and-ha-ha-Simmy-gets-to-eat-whatever-she-wants-now smile. "You don't see many opera singers touring with French horn players."

Sheikh Zafir beamed down at me. "I'll have Mrs. Farahani arrange a solo concert, then. Well done, Simmy." He looked back at the crowd. "And now that we've settled the matter, let us begin the auction."

He turned his attention to the front of the room, where a small stage was set up. An auctioneer began the bidding for a well-known painting, and the incident was forgotten.

"I think my big sister would be good friends with yours," Queen Raelena whispered to me. "Oh, I'll have to show you my elephant collection! And I know just the place to find a duck brooch. Although, I see you more as a swan."

If it hadn't been against every social rule in every world culture, I would have jumped on her back and hugged her for infinity. "Thank you. I look forward to it greatly."

She bowed and I dipped my head. Once she was gone, I stuck Simmy's French horn under my arm. "I'd better go put this back in my room," I said to a shocked Nabila. "Don't want another"—I made quotation marks with my fingers—"'accident' to happen to it."

I skipped my way through all twenty-eight hallways. The bubble pulsated on Simmy's bed, most probably from Meredith's impatience. I tore off a sheet of paper from Simmy's duck stationery and wrote a quick sub report.

Dear Princess Simmy,

Stick with Queen Raelena. She's totally genuine (unlike your sister—you weren't kidding there) and dedicated to helping out ALL women. Plus, she's QUEEN RAELENA! Sorry if you get nervous about performing, but it was a tricky situation, and now people will hear your awesome playing loud and clear. So just be yourself, duck-loving and all. And if Nabila acts really mean around you—well, meaner—it's because I/you/we showed her up. You outshine her, Simmy. Stand tall. It was an honor to know you, er, be you.

Hugs,
Desi

P.S. Sorry about your horn, but trust me, it was for the best.

Chapter

11

"What a rush." I plopped down on the couch and waited for the rouge to change me back. "And I totally nailed it."

"Nailed it?" Meredith sounded angry.

I rolled over to face her.

"Stuck a nail in your coffin, maybe. *Desi*. Offering to do concerts? Mouthing off to her sister? The poor introverted mouse is going to swoon when she gets home."

"She's more duck than mouse."

Meredith didn't smile.

"Meredith, I did great! Here." I clicked through the manual and leaned on her desk to show her. "Look at Simmy's 'About Me' thing. She wanted to give Nabila a piece of her mind. Check. She likes to play the French horn. Check. And I even found her a kindred spirit. I rocked it!"

Meredith sighed and folded her arms. "Believe me, I know how tempting it is to go in and fix things for these girls, but usually it creates more of a mess."

"How?" I challenged.

Instead of answering, Meredith started typing. "Please get off my desk. It's African teak, you know."

I slid down and hopped over to her window. I'd never looked out before. Craziness. It was like being in a plane, except the clouds were zipping by at warp speed.

"You know what I still don't get?" I asked.

"Everything?"

"How you can get from Paris to the Arabian Peninsula in thirty minutes."

"You mix magic with science and"—she snapped—"possibility." She made a final mouse click and turned to face me. "I have news."

"Ow!" I dropped the manual on the couch. "It zapped me!"

"Just a friendly you've-got-mail alert," she said. "Because lucky for you, an assignment just came in, and there's no one else to fill it."

"Don't you need my Princess Progress Report first?" I asked. "I thought we'd review it and I could take a little break."

"Well, you might say things are a little backed up in

Hank's department right now, poor guy. Those computers have taken on a life of their own. The PPR will wait, and this *is* your break. So sit. Read."

Hand still buzzing, I clicked open my newest message. There wasn't a headshot of the princess, just a picture of a leering tribal mask. I suspected this girl had never had a picture taken in her life.

PRINCESS AMA YAKINOMI

Age: 14

Hometown: Ticuna tribe/ Western Amazon

Favorite Color: Moss green

Favorite Food: Fried sloth arms. Three-toed are best.

Favorite Book: Book?

Family Background: My father is Chief Yakinomi. I have three brothers, but they live in the tent of the males. I have a caretaker—Kopenawa.

Cultural Traditions: I have remained in this jungle since birth. We have followed the fatherly traditions for a very long time.

Anything Else We Should Know: I became a woman a few months before, and thence began my isolation period to study our traditions. Except, I snuck out, which you must not tell unless you want me to come for you with a blow dart.

Before I left for the isolation I had great fight with my father because I fear this change and because I have to marry soon and I desire that I had a selection, but I do not.

109

At the ceremony a husband will select me. So when I sneak away, I was on walk and utter wondering, what if I could leave for some time before I make all these big selections? Then I saw an auspicious bird—and confessed to the bird the desires of my heart. It was a good thing, because an orb appeared and disgorged a woman who told me I can enjoy a holiday because I have magic inside me. (This I knew already. The chief's daughter encloses the village's magic.) Thus I will have a turn of the world outside my own. Hope I packed in the best way. And good fortune to you during your employment.

Okay, that was an *awful* translation—maybe the very first English translation of the tribe's language—but I got the basics. Ama was a Level One princess who probably wouldn't even know about the agency if she didn't have some MP herself. She wanted to get out of the jungle for a while and needed help with this ceremony, whatever it was. Not something Lilith would be impressed with, but so what? How often do you get to visit the Amazon? The most exotic place I'd been before subbing was the Hogle Zoo in Salt Lake. They didn't even have a three-toed sloth there.

My rouge compact beeped, and the twenty-minute countdown began. While I waited, I searched the manual for "Ticuna tribe," and nothing came up. I broadened my search to "Amazon" and found a couple of uh-oh tidbits: some tribes had been observed to communicate telepathically. Fantastic. The rouge couldn't help me there. And worse, many tribes had never been observed AT ALL. So no one knew what kind of reactions they might have to, say, a fake princess.

To calm my nerves I put a search in on Prince Barrett and flipped through some of his latest pictures. I wondered if I could cut out Floressa Chase and Photoshop myself in her place. Wait, forget Photoshop. Try princess swap. I was so fixated on the idea that I didn't notice we'd landed until Meredith clucked her tongue.

"Is this assignment totally normal?" I asked, focusing my attention back to the task at hand and shutting off the manual. "I mean, the agency doesn't seem to have much info on this one. Have you met Ama?"

"No, that was Genevieve. Found her so charming, she took this assignment pro bono and delegated it to me. She's experimental like that," Meredith said distractedly, then grumbled something about cloning herself. "Oh drat! Look, I have to go. I can't help you with everything. That info is plenty—one little ceremony and then I'll be back to get you later today, tomorrow tops. After that you can take some time to rest. Now scoot."

I stepped through the bubble onto the mossy jungle floor. A thin stream of sunlight seeped through the trees, but the forest was so dense it was hard to guess the time. The loud mix of birdcalls and insect hums was overwhelming, but the humidity was worse—I couldn't tell where my sweat ended and the jungle mist began.

I waited under the cover of the jungle while I transformed. In the sweltering heat I hardly felt more than a twinge as I shrunk a good eight inches and my skin color darkened. I went to shove my hands into my pockets, but felt only skin. I was wearing nothing but a yellow beaded necklace, some paint, and, I guessed, a look of pure mortification.

Which meant I didn't have a pocket or purse to hide the rouge and manual in. If I got caught with these, there'd be some questions to answer. I shot a few mean voodoo thoughts in Meredith's direction, then hid my things under a red-flowered bush, and stepped back. Hm. There were *tons* of bushes with red flowers. I grabbed some stones and made a big arrow on the jungle floor, pointing to my treasures, and backed slowly into a clearing.

About a hundred feet ahead of me lay a vast circle of tree-leaf huts: Ama's village. Drums pounded in the distance, accompanied by the occasional whoop or shout. Gradually the words began to make sense. *Ceremony, fire,* and *spirit.*

"Ama!" An old woman emerged from one of the huts and wagged her finger at me, making me grateful I'd already stashed my stuff. Her graying hair was cut long with blunt bangs across her forehead. The red in her simple wrap-style skirt matched the paint on her face and stomach. She wasn't wearing a shirt. And by the looks of things, she'd never worn a bra either. "The sun is almost directly overhead. We must prepare you before the ceremony begins. Thoughtless girl." She shuffled into a conical, thatched-roof hut, and I followed her inside. A few rope hammocks hung from load-bearing logs, and the dirt floor was hard and smooth.

"Sorry I wasn't here," I said, eyeing a pile of furry fabric spread across a dark wood table. "Are those my clothes, um . . ." Ama had mentioned a name. What was it? "Ma'am?"

"Ma'am? Why are you being so formal? I don't understand."

"Oh, instead of your name, I thought I'd call you that. Uh, for respect."

She laughed. "I think your isolation may have jumbled your brain. You've called me Kopenawa your entire life. Now lie down and I'll get the scissors."

I gulped. "Scissors?"

"Unless you want me to do it the ancient way and pull out all of your hair strand by strand. You might want to rest during it too. Store up some energy for what's to come."

What's to come? Scissors and nudity. Here's a philosophical question: If a sub yells in a rain forest and there's no agent around to hear her, does she really make a sound?

My mom was the beauty queen, my dad was the hardworking lawyer, Gracie was the living baby doll, and I . . . I was the perseverer. I didn't quit. Even when I got the muckiest of muck jobs. Even when I didn't make the school play in sixth grade, I thought, what the heck, I'll try out again. It was for a role in *Cats*, so part of the audition was a feline gymnastics routine. I fell down in the middle of a simple cartwheel. Not a round off or a back handspring. A cartwheel. Everyone laughed, and I think the director even snorted.

And at that moment, the moment where my body was twisted in all sorts of unflattering angles—my shirt flipped up and my ponytail barely hanging on—I was at least reassured with the knowledge that I could never again experience humiliation so awful.

Of course, I hadn't foreseen a workaholic princess agent sending me ALONE to the Amazon rain forest to have all my hair removed, my body covered in black paint and eagle feathers, and a whole village of expectant, indigenous people waiting for me to make my passage into adulthood by performing some sort of dance I didn't know.

Kopenawa led me to a crowded hut about half the size of my school cafeteria. A pit of fire blazed in the middle, with two half-naked men (more like three-quarters naked. Grass skirts don't hide much) standing next to it. Even more men set up drums at the edge of the hut. They were talking about me—apparently neighboring villagers had traveled here just for this ceremony, to see if the chief's daughter would make a good wife.

Great. This girl's whole future rested on whatever was going to happen next. If I messed this up, no guy would choose her for a wife. This was the kind of impact I wasn't sure I wanted to be involved in. I turned to Kopenawa. "I can't do this."

"You can, and you will make Chief Yakinomi proud. Do the dance well, and you can have any man out there as your husband."

"Really?" I asked, confused.

"Oh, your father was just angry before. Once he sees how hard you try, he will give you a say. You'll see."

"Right. But I'm still not clear what this dance is."

Kopenawa laughed again. "Really, you are too funny. You can do this dance in your sleep. You've had four months to prepare. Think of the traditions you've learned, the ancestors you follow. You dance for them as well. Make it memorable."

A guy a few years older than me, with nice biceps, broke free of the crowd and grabbed my hand. "Good luck, Ama," he said, giving my hand a gentle squeeze. When we touched I got a tingling, warm, happy feeling, and wondered if it was my MP telling me something about this guy. Could he be the one for Ama?

"Uh, thank you," I said. Behind him, a muscled, middle-aged man with a stern expression and lots and lots of feathers frowned at me. The feathers gave him an air of importance, like he was the chief or something. Ama's dad? Yikes. I shot him a peace-making "Hi, Dad" sort of smile, figuring it couldn't hurt to ease the tension a little. A look of surprise crossed his hard face, and his eyes softened for a second. Then he pounded the ground with his staff, nearly scaring the MP out of me, and the drums began to beat. The next thing I knew, two men grabbed my arms and carried me into a circle, chanting in a soft hum. They led me to the fire and took a step back. I looked to Kopenawa for a hint.

"Jump," she whispered.

I jumped over the flames, the heat licking my heels. The

crowd picked up the chanting, which evolved into a song peppered with animal calls.

Animal calls. That's right. We watched an Amazon tribal ceremony video in World History last spring. We had to bring permission slips to watch it because of the revealing clothes. The video said animal calls were a good thing. Then again, some of the traditions involved guys sticking their hands in gloves filled with fire ants, and women piercing their faces. This ceremony had better stop with the fire jumping.

"Jump again," Kopenawa mouthed.

So I jumped again. And again. And again. The noises grew louder and wilder, filling the hut, filling the forest. I jumped for what must have been hours, and as I did, villagers came and went, like it was halftime at a college football game. I saw the hand-squeeze guy having a solemn conversation with Ama's dad.

My feet blistered from the heat. Faces appeared in the flames. Meredith, my parents, Celeste, Hayden, Kylee. It's not like they spoke or gave me wisdom. They just stared with these blank expressions, like they weren't sure if I'd succeed.

A whole village watched, yet my motivation came from those faces. If those people were here—if they could see me now—well, first of all, they'd flip. But once they got over the shock of Desi Bascomb performing a tribal ritual on behalf of the chief's daughter, they'd see I was made of something more solid than the smoke rising toward the jungle sky.

Finally the drums stopped and a leathered elder, also

painted black, extinguished the flames. You'd think things couldn't get much worse than a fire dance, but then two masked figures appeared, circling around me and hissing.

Kopenawa shook her head. "Dance."

I was desperate to rest, but I closed my eyes.

Dance.

The oldest dance I knew was the Pony, and that was only from the 1960s. Eyes still closed, I started with that, throwing in a few twists and twirls. I picked up the rhythm from the drums and coiled my body in ways it'd never gone before. I rolled my stomach like a belly dancer, then lifted up my knees like I'd seen on my mom's kickboxing videos. Energy exploded from every pore. I WAS an Amazon princess.

Until I opened my eyes and saw the alarmed expressions on the villagers' faces. The drums stopped and someone coughed, which even in the depths of the rain forest meant I'd bombed the ceremony. The chief started toward me, carrying his stick, which had a spearhead . . . made of some kind of bone. I didn't know what the punishment was for failing a Becoming a Woman Dance, but I wasn't going to stick around and find out if the tribe resorted to cannibalism.

So I ran.

Chapter
I2

There's a reason sports bras are made out of tight-fitting Lycra and not eagle feathers. My chest hurt. My feet throbbed. But most of all, my head felt like it was going to explode.

What was I doing? I'd just ruined this poor girl's life— the only husband she was going to get now would be some foul-smelling reject who got kicked off hunting duty because he couldn't handle a blow dart. Or worse, she'd be shunned and left to the dangers of the Amazon.

But then again, if this was such a big deal for the girl, why'd she leave? Why leave some random substitute to perform a life-defining ceremony while you tour the world bubble-style? That wasn't how a princess should act. She should face the problem, chin up. How could these girls not realize what an awesome responsibility they had? They couldn't just run away from their problems like . . . well, like I just did.

I stopped running and doubled over, gasping for air. Vapor was better than this. As my breathing slowed, it occurred to me that I was a scapegoat. The reason the princesses didn't have to face these scary moments was because they had me. But I didn't have anyone who could jump in and change everything for me. I was still alone.

A startled bird squawked at me from a tree, reminding me that I was perfectly visible. I needed to hide until Meredith showed up, however long that was.

The rouge! I had to find my stuff or I wouldn't have a clue when the princess was on her way back. Scratch that. I had to *make* her come back. No way was I going to just wait here with bugs and jungle creatures eyeing me for lunch. But my hiding place could be anywhere. Everything looked the same.

I sat down on a mossy log and pulled my knees to my chest. The black paint was already smearing where I'd sweat. I gave my armpit a quick sniff. *Ew.*

"What are you doing?"

A girl about my age, dressed in a short skirt and a HITCHING A RIDE T-shirt, stood beside me, holding a woven bag. "Aren't you my sub?"

"I am. Well, I was." I rose from the log and towered over her.

"You're taller than me. I thought you'd be exactly my size."

She was right. I was taller. My body still looked like hers for the most part, but I could feel my limbs slowly stretching out. "I don't have my compact, so I didn't know you were coming back. Besides, I think my height is the least of your worries. I think I just kind of . . . messed it up."

"Did you fall into the fire pit? Every time I thought about doing the ceremony, the fire pit scared me."

"No. The dance did me in."

"Oh, don't worry about the dance. It's not as symbolic as the rest of it. The fire part proves I'm ready for adulthood. The rest is mostly for show."

I pursed my lips. My heart was still beating fast, but now it was from the anger welling inside of me. How could she be so casual about the whole thing? "Well, no offense, but if the fire hopping and everything else is such a big deal, why did you leave? I mean, you had months of isolation to prepare. How was I supposed to walk in and do a decent job?"

"Well, you did it, right? It will work out fine. Besides, my father is chief. I'm not going to get punished because you could not complete your obligation."

"Whether or not I could finish the obligation isn't what I'm talking about here." I folded my arms across my still-bare chest. "Being royalty is a privilege you shouldn't take lightly."

The girl tugged at her shirt before finally tearing it off. "How do you wear those clothes?" She poked through her bag, pulling out a pot of black paint, which she began smear-ing on her body to match me.

"Look, I'm not trying to lecture you." I analyzed my toes while she continued to paint herself. It's hard to look someone in the eyes when they're shirtless. "I know it's not my place to say this, but running away isn't going to solve the problem, you know? You left a huge mess for me to wade through."

Ama groaned. "I know. I didn't mean to. I . . . got scared. After this ceremony, I'm an adult. I have to get married to whomever my father chooses, even if I don't like him. I just wanted to see what else was out there before all these changes happen. Does that make sense?"

More than you know. I swatted a bug on the back of my neck. I drew my hand back to see a squished mosquito the size of a rodent. *Get me out of here.* "Yeah. That must be hard. Wait—Kopenawa told me your dad was just mad when he said you didn't have a choice."

Ama looked astonished. "Really? She said that?"

"Yeah. And there was a nice-looking guy who wished you good luck. He talked to your dad."

"Did he have strong arms and a nice smile?"

"Yep."

"That was Tereis. You saw Tereis talking to my dad?"

"I think so. But then after the dance your dad came toward me with a spear. That's when I took off."

Ama laughed. "My dad always has his spear. He wasn't going to hurt you. He would never hurt me." She glanced back at her village. "Look, my people are kind and forgiving. I'll just go back and explain I had doubts during the ceremony, but a wise tree spirit enlightened me. You can't argue with a tree spirit."

Tree spirit. Yet another title *not* in the job description.

Ama brought out some scissors from the bag, and we got to work hacking off her hair.

Our task was briefly interrupted by the most beautiful sound in the world. A humming that wasn't a giant insect. A bubble appeared, barely visible behind a tangle of vines. It looked different—smaller—with an actual door.

I raised my arms to the Amazon gods. Let there be bubble.

"Hey, that's like the orb I traveled in!" Ama said as I finished the final snips. "And the things I saw! Have you ever seen a *car*? And I had no idea there were so many kinds of food!" She sighed. "I'm glad I had a chance to see it, but now I'm ready to go back. So, thanks."

"Oh, you're welc—"

Something whirred by my head, and Ama jumped away. A dart had lodged in my bubble, which was now shooting neon-green sparks.

"So much for the tree spirit," Princess Ama said.

"Huh? What?" Another dart pierced my bubble. "Why are they bursting my bubble?"

"Two identical-looking princesses standing next to each other equals evil spirits."

"But they shouldn't be able to see the bubble. Unless . . .

Oh great. I bet you *all* have MP!"

"Well, get out of here! Those darts are poisonous; you'll be seeing evil spirits yourself soon."

"Okay, well . . ." I wanted to end this "Kumbaya" moment on a high note. "Peace be unto you."

"What?" Ama yelled.

"Bye!" I pushed the bubble door open and stumbled in. Instead of Meredith's office, there was a jetlike cockpit with flashing sirens and the sign EMERGENCY BUBBLE lit above.

"Warning! Warning! Bubble malfunction!" said a robotic voice.

"No!" I pounded the green GO button. "I have to get out of here! I don't even have my manual!"

The bubble choked and rose into the air, tossing me up, down, and around. It flew for about ten seconds before the voice said, "Bubble is unable to function and will self-destruct in ten seconds. Please vacate the bubble immediately. Your agent has been contacted and another bubble will be sent."

"There's flying darts out there. Where do I go?"

"Out is a good option. You have five seconds. Four, three . . ."

I crawled through the bubble door, not knowing how far I would fall. I flew through some tree branches and thorny leaves before crashing onto the forest floor. Oy. Ow. Ouch. One of those snapping sounds on the way down wasn't a branch. It was a rib.

The floating bubble was just visible through the hole my body had made in the branches on my descent. The pitch of the bubble's hiss increased, piercing my eardrums. Just when I thought the sound couldn't get any higher, there was a soft popping and the bubble disappeared, leaving a puff of purple smoke.

I sucked in short gasps of air, clutching my side. "Help!" I sobbed. "Please, mighty tree spirits, if you can hear me! Help!"

Chapter
13

"Tree spirits? Oh, please."

I squinted through the agony. My super-understanding and empathetic agent had come to save me.

"It's one rib. Maybe two." Meredith wiped some slime from her brown crocodile boots. Her green A-line skirt, white blouse, and enormous sunglasses were more New Yorker than Amazon adventurer, but the heat didn't faze her. "Once, I broke both legs in a malfunctioning bubble crash. Here." She plucked a gnarled stick out of her green briefcase and waved it over me. The pain eased.

"Magic wand?" I spit out a bug.

"Amazon healing stick. Useful little souvenir." She pulled me up and led me into her bubble. It was the most beautiful sight I'd ever seen, although I could have done without the chartreuse. I'd gone greener than Greenpeace in that jungle.

"You can sit at my desk."

"I'd rather lie down."

"Fine. But try not to bleed or throw up on the uphol-stery. It's Italian and I just got it cleaned."

Ignoring her, I collapsed onto the couch. "I hope I earned a break before the next job. Where are we going anyway?"

"*We* aren't going anywhere. *You* are going home."

"Really? When's my next assignment?"

"You really think I'm giving you another job after that disaster? Leaving the gig before I got there is bad enough, but destroying an emergency bubble is in clear violation of Item Six of your contract. Oh, and I found your manual and rouge. Anyone could have, thanks to your arrow, which would have been yet *another* mess to clean up."

"Um, hello? I was naked! No private, safe places. What did you want me to do with my stuff? And I didn't destroy a bubble! It malfunctioned! They were shooting blow darts at me. The contract said mortal danger is an exception, remember?"

Meredith fixed me with a hard stare. "But you did run out of that village early. Got spotted with your client. True, you didn't have your timer, but that emergency bubble got there fast enough. You would have been fine if you hadn't hung around chatting. Luckily, the villagers believed you were a spirit, and you got off without a Sub Spotting on your record. But the blow darts wouldn't have happened if you'd done your job. So it's on you."

On me. *On me?* I'm a responsible teenager. I got a job before I'd even started high school. I do my homework every night. I help old ladies cross the street. I brush AND floss. I am willing to accept when I make a bad choice, like the time I wore leggings with my SPROUTVILLE SUPERHERO shirt and everyone called me Captain Toothpick for a week. But I was not about to take responsibility for this.

"So we'll agree to disagree on the bubble thing. I still think . . . I want to stay, Meredith. Please."

"You're a liability, Desi. Shaking things up for Simmy, and now running away from the village and right into your client? *Talking* to her?"

"Of course I ran. You said we don't do major life moments, and there I was doing a Becoming a Woman tribal dance."

Meredith looked up and rubbed her chin. "That was a translation error. We thought you were going to a *trivial* dance."

"What? No! I had the whole village there. And based on what Ama said, I probably did it right. Which is pretty tough considering there was fire! And—"

"Stop. You made mistakes. Big mistakes." She shook her head. "I'm going to have to think about this. I still haven't made up my mind about you. I've got to go back to the agency now and sort out this bubble business. In the meantime, I'm putting you on probation. Go home and think about the rules and see if this is something you can really do.

I'll be in touch and let you know what I've decided, but don't get your hopes up."

I hunched my shoulders, collapsing into my failure. She made me sound, like, incompetent. I mean, okay, so maybe I shouldn't have assumed Ama's dad was going to kill me. And I could see how talking to the princess might be a problem. But what would Ama have done without me, really? I still believed this was something I could do. That maybe I had a talent for understanding people and making a difference in their lives. An impact.

But the Celeste Junipers of the world were right: Desi Bascomb isn't *that* girl. The only thing to do was go home and try to make my regular life as tolerable as possible.

I clenched my jaw. I wouldn't let Meredith see me cry. "How long until we're home?"

The bubble thumped.

"Ask and you shall receive." Meredith pointed to the door without even bothering to wave good-bye.

Fine. It was a pleasure doing business with you too.

I walked right back into my bathroom. The floor was still wet. I touched the water. Warm. If my ribs hadn't been sore, I might have convinced myself nothing had ever happened.

It was only seven thirty according to the clock in my bedroom, but I didn't care. I slumped into my bed and slept. Forget a pea—not even an invading army could wake this princess.

Ahem. Former princess.

Chapter
14

"Desi. Wake up. We have to go."

I squeezed my eyes shut. Did I *ever* get to sleep on this job? Where was Meredith taking me now that I'd crashed the . . . Wait. My eyes fluttered open. There was a woman in a tiara hovering over me. I yelped and tumbled out of bed.

"Honey! What is wrong with you?"

I rubbed my eyes. My room came into focus, as did my mom, decked out in a black sequined evening gown and pink lipstick. Gracie squirmed in her arms.

"Des, I need to be on the Idaho Beauties of the Past car in forty-five minutes, and I have to get Gracie into her pioneer dress for the costume contest."

"The parade? That's today?"

Mom stopped patting Gracie's back for a second and pulled me up. "June twenty-eighth. Same weekend it's been every year since 1910."

"Right. It's June twenty-eighth. And yesterday was the twenty-seventh. I worked yesterday. I took a bath yesterday."

"Are you feeling okay?" Mom smoothed my hair out of my face. "Oh honey, you look awful." She puckered her lips. "All right. Go grab my under-eye cream, the volumizing mascara, and my pink eye shadow. I know you don't like makeup, but I'm giving you a five-minute quick fix."

"Who said I don't like makeup?"

"Well, you never wear it."

"No one has ever shown me how to put it on," I said.

"Don't be silly. I showed you the basics in charm school."

"That was Celeste. I gouged my eye with the mascara wand, so you had me hold the curling iron while you made up her face."

Gracie rested her chin on Mom's shoulder, the perfect mommy-daughter pair. Sometimes I wondered if Celeste should be in the family instead of me. They could do catalog ads, or life insurance commercials together.

Mom readjusted a stray bobby pin. "Get some blush too. You look pale."

Blush. Rouge. I almost laughed. I'd just danced in the Amazon rain forest, and now I was arguing over beauty products with my mom.

I found Mom's makeup on top of Grandma's hand-me-down bureau and dug through the bulging bag for the blush.

Good thing my mom wasn't like Meredith, who'd probably pluck out my eyebrows, just for fun. Although Meredith did have style, I'll give her that. That skirt she'd worn the other day was totally Audrey.

Gosh, why was I even *thinking* about Meredith? I. WAS. HOME. Princessing was O-VER.

So why'd I have to feel so, I don't know, unfinished?

I actually did feel better after Mom worked her makeup magic in a record three minutes. She parted my hair on the side and twisted it into two loose braids. "More flattering for your facial structure," she said. Translation—the swoop covered up my big forehead.

She patted my shoulder and gazed at us in the mirror. "You're prettier than all the float girls combined."

"Yeah, right," I said, a bit harsher than I'd intended. "I mean, I'm just tired of being compared to them."

Mom flinched. "You don't need a tiara to be beautiful, honey. I hope you know that. Beauty comes from embracing who you are."

Easy for her to say. Mom telling me looks don't matter was like a millionaire telling a homeless guy that money isn't everything. No way she really believed it.

"I'd better get changed," I said.

Mom paused, like she wanted to say more, but smoothed over the tension with her usual sunshine. "All right, then. See you in five minutes?"

You know how when you've been on a boat or an

airplane and get back on solid ground and still feel that rocking sensation? That's what being home felt like. I had magic in me, I'd used it, and I could still feel tingles of it. And the reminder hurt, knowing what I had the capacity to do and not being sure if I'd ever get another chance.

I rummaged absently through my closet, settling on a vintage, brown, knee-length skirt. I'd already designed my shirt for the event—aqua blue with the state of Idaho on it, and IDAHO DAZE spelled out in cursive letters. I'd printed my Web site on the back in the hopes of scoring a few Internet hits.

We made it to State Street just in time for Mom to slip into a 1964 yellow Mustang. She stretched her arms and cracked her neck, prepping for the next hour of elbow, elbow, wrist, wrist waving. Mom was one of the parade highlights every year—winning Miss Idaho and placing fourth in Miss America was the closest to stardom anyone in this town had ever gotten.

Unless you counted Jasper Gomez, who made national news when he tried to steal every set of Mickey Mouse ears from Disneyland but ended up getting knocked out by Daisy Duck. Jasper didn't get to ride in a car, which would actually be hard, being as he's in prison.

So, yeah, Mom is the star, and then there's me.

The pooper-scooper.

Drake was lounging by the lemonade stand, eating some brownies he'd brought from home. "Want one?" he asked when I tapped him on the back.

"Uh, I'll pass."

"Your loss." He pointed to a wagon stenciled with the Pets Charming logo. "You gonna be Gladys today?"

I motioned to my skirt and turquoise ballet flats. "No, I don't want to get sweaty. And my mom did my makeup."

Drake snorted, spraying some brownie crumbs into his goatee, and reached for the shovel leaning against the wagon. "Then here's your shovel, my lady. Hopefully you won't get any manure on your shoes."

My stomach tightened at the "my lady" line. If only he knew where I'd been and what I'd lost.

"Desi!" Kylee waved from the grass outside of 7-Eleven.

So we were still talking, at least. "I'll see ya, Drake."

Drake bit into another brownie. "Cool. You're at the end, by the way, after some big fancy truck. Oh, and after the parade, do you mind working at our booth?"

"Do I get overtime?"

Drake laughed, coughing up more brownie. Guess that was a no. Ah, well. Money is money, whether it's a melio or minimum wage.

I dodged a rodeo clown and made my way to the band. Instruments squeaked as a few kids began tuning. The French horn player made me wince.

Kylee sat crossed-legged, sucking on her clarinet reed, her black hair arranged in its usual messy bun. She looked cute in khaki shorts and the REAL MUSICIANS SPIT shirt I'd made her for Christmas. I plopped down in the grass and grabbed a chocolate doughnut from the open box next to her. "So."

Kylee slid her reed out. "So."

I bit into my doughnut. I so wished I could tell Kylee about my princess adventures. She'd totally be on my side on the whole Ama situation. Plus, holding in a secret like that felt like I'd been underwater for minutes, and the only way to get air was to tell the truth.

But she'd never believe it. I mean, the girl fact-checked our history textbook, not to mention what she would say about the whole contract—

Stop. Get over it, Desi. No more thinking about subbing.

"I was drama yesterday," I said.

"Yeah, you were." She sighed. "But I guess I was too. And we don't even have time to fight anyway. Not when there is *that* development to discuss."

She pointed at the concession stand, where a tall dark-haired boy stood talking animatedly with the high school principal, Mrs. Davies. It was easy to see she was totally charmed. For one, the guy had her in tears with some funny story, and I'd never even seen her smile before. His tan skin, curly dark hair, and athletic build only added to his charm. He noticed Kylee and me watching him and broke into a devastatingly cute smile. A little zing went off inside me, like the manual jolt that came with princess mail. I ducked my head.

"He just smiled at you," Kylee said.

"And you too. Wait, is that—?"

"The new kid. His name is Reed Pearson. Kyrsti Devon

134

talked to him at the post office yesterday and said his accent is adorable AND he's nice, which would officially make him a celestial being and a Sproutville, I don't know, *endangered species*."

"Hey, Hayden's nice!"

"When?"

I shook my head. No amount of convincing would change her mind about Hayden. Besides, there was no denying it. This Reed guy was cute. Cute enough that he might pique Celeste's interest and leave Hayden to me. Not that I wanted Celeste to snag Reed, but still. I'd take any window I could when it came to Hayden. "Let's file Hayden under the topics-we-don't-discuss category, okay?"

"Fine by me. But Reed should be fair game—Hey, he's looking over here again. At you. Desi, he's totally staring at you. You've never talked to him, have you? Ran into him at the mall or something?"

I didn't look up. "Of course not. I've never even seen him before."

A bullhorn sounded, meaning we had five minutes to get into place.

Kylee screwed her clarinet together and blew a pitch-perfect note. "Well, I hope Celeste isn't on the do-not-discuss list, because I really need to point out how wrong that dress is."

She nodded at a ridiculously souped-up truck covered in fake pink and purple flowers. Celeste stood in the middle of it, her Miss Sproutville Spud Princess sash on her chest, a

Vaselined smile already in place. Her underwear lines glared inside her red spandexy dress.

"Do you think guys notice how tacky she is? Seriously, I don't get it," Kylee said.

I groaned. "Well, I get to watch her the whole way."

"Why? Trucks don't poo."

"No, but the horses behind them do. This is so humiliating."

As if on cue, a set of Clydesdales clopped into line. And wouldn't you know it, Hayden Garrison, in a blue vintage cowboy shirt and boot-cut jeans, was already saddled on to one of them.

Just like our version of a mall, "parade" is a very big word to describe a very small-town event. It started with kids in pioneer costumes riding their bikes while throwing candy at the crowd. I don't know where this tradition began—I doubted the Mormon pioneers, starved and fatigued, had had much of anything to offer when they'd arrived in Idaho, let alone candy. But that was just the start. Next up were the marching bands—from junior high to the Elks lodge. The floats, all six of them, rolled out next. The first three were homemade oddities, chicken wire wrapped around old trailers and stuffed with napkins, some of which fell off. The county made the only one worthy of being called a "float," and it carried every important county official, including my dad, dressed up as different Idaho heroes—from cowboys to Olympians. A rainbow arched over the float congregation, symbolizing a better tomorrow or yesterday or some garbage like that. Next came the convertibles and trucks, with the horses rounding out the fun.

I don't know any of this firsthand because I didn't actually SEE any of the parade. I'm constructing it from past memories. My parade view was Hayden, which would have been a lovely forty-five-minute diversion if I hadn't been scooping the nastiness that came out of his horse's backside. But Hayden did turn around once and wave at me. I would have scooped all the poop in the world for a moment like that.

When the parade of poo was over, I beelined to the Pets Charming truck and chucked my shovel into the back. I wiped my hands on my skirt and looked up to see Hayden five feet away at the horse trailer. He nodded at me as he handed his uncle the horse's reins. "Hey, Daisy," he said.

"Desi. Hey. Um . . . hay!" I pointed to the bale of hay inside the trailer. "Hay-den."

Hayden's expression went blank.

Note to self: avoid using awful puns as icebreakers. "So, that parade was fun."

"Uh-huh. How'd you get stuck with the shovel?"

"I've been asking myself that same question all day."

Hayden laughed a little. "Dirty job, but someone's got to do it, right?"

"Yep."

He squinted at my shirt. "You spelled *days* wrong on your shirt."

"I didn't, well, yeah I did, but I meant to. It's a play on words." Why was it so hard for me to talk to him? Connect, Desi, connect. This is your chance. "Don't you like a good play on words? Or playing? With . . . words?"

Hayden's blank look was back, tinged with skepticism. "You mean, like games?"

I breathed out. "Yeah. Like word games."

"Dude, I love word games." He listed on his fingers. "Scrabble or word searches or . . ."

"Boggle?" I didn't say the word, more like singsonged it.

"Yeah. Hey, remember when we used to play it online when we were kids? Boggle."

"I still play sometimes, if you ever want to."

"That'd be cool. It's been a while since . . . you know. I did things like that."

We stood there for a moment, neither one saying anything. Maybe we were destined to have one of those agonizing romances like in the Audrey Hepburn movie *Sabrina*—girl is right there, guy doesn't see, but after she comes back from Paris, she's all he wants. I mean, he'd remembered our past, now he just needed to see through my vapor, see the girl—

"Hey." Celeste walked up to Hayden and pressed her spandex dress into him. She spoke to him like I wasn't there. Like I didn't even exist. "We're all over at the pie tent. You coming?"

"Uh-huh," he said. Celeste looped her arm around his waist and veered him toward the festivities.

I glared at the open sky, so much bluer than the fake one at The Venetian, wishing it could swallow me whole. First my job, now my crush. Tears stung my eyes, but I choked them back.

"Hey." Hayden had stopped walking. He was looking right at me. So was Celeste. She couldn't ignore me now. "You wanna come too?"

"Sure!" I said. "I'll, uh, meet you there in a bit. I have to go . . . talk to someone first."

"Cool." Hayden turned back, his arm hanging over Celeste's bare shoulder. She looked furious, which only made me giddier.

I had to go pretend I had something important to do for the next five minutes and then, THEN I was going to eat blue-ribbon pie with Hayden Garrison.

And, well, his girlfriend—my ex–best friend.

Chapter
15

I raced through the parking lot for the next seven minutes, trying to blow off some of the adrenaline pumping through me. It had happened. That moment. With Hayden. I was different now, surely he had noticed it.

So he still messed up my name. And he'd walked away with Celeste. But I was so close, closer than ever.

I checked my reflection in the side-view mirror of a minivan. Makeup still on. Forehead still covered. I smoothed my already sweating hands on my skirt and tried my best not to skip into the fair.

Celeste and the HMs were circled around the pie sample table. There were seven girls total, looking like a jar of jellybeans in their different colored camisoles. I'd never been friends with four of them—they were seventh graders Celeste had recruited and would probably dump next year—but Annie (blue) and Nikki (orange) had been my friends before the big split. We hadn't talked since then, but they still smiled at me sometimes in the halls, when Celeste wasn't there.

"Where's Hayden?" Nikki lifted her curly brunette mane off her shoulders and fanned her neck.

"His mom said he had to take his brother on a ride first." Celeste twirled her hair around her finger. "I'm so glad I don't have to hang out with my family."

I scooted closer to their table. You know, just the day before I'd have sold my T-shirt collection to be in their camisole club. Which seemed silly now that I'd danced the Pony for blow-dart enthusiasts and hung out at a charity dinner with Queen Raelena, not to mention my little stint as a celebrity, even if it was an insect one.

Still, there was history with these girls. Secrets and inside jokes and laughter that I hadn't been a part of since the split. Part of me, a big part of me, wanted it back, Celeste and all.

I lingered by the raspberry pie, waiting for a chance to break into the circle. My nerves crackled. Stupid! Why couldn't I say two words to a group of girls who used to be my friends?

I was NOT vapor. I focused all my energy, all my insecurities and hope and courage into my pointer finger and tapped Nikki on the back.

She almost gasped when she whirled around. "Desi!" Her eyes darted to Celeste, then back to me. "How are you?"

"Great! You?"

"Really good." She paused, perhaps to see if Celeste would interrupt. "Your hair looks cute like that."

Celeste crossed her arms, her lips forming a tight line, but said nothing.

Nikki's smile grew. "I saw your mom. Her dress is so hot. My mom never wears anything but mom jeans."

"Thanks." The compliment brought me strength. I had to remind them how things had been before they'd decided I was invisible. "Hey, remember in fourth grade when we snuck into my mom's closet and dressed up in her gowns?"

Annie giggled like she'd been holding it in for two years. "Oh. My. Gosh! I totally remember that! That was so much fun! Remember when Nikki got stuck in a spaghetti strap?"

Nikki elbowed Annie. "Well, you put your dress on backwards."

"I still have pictures of that!" I laughed.

Nikki covered her mouth. "You don't!"

The other HMs broke the circle, forming a straight line in front of the table. They gave me the once-over, shoes to hair, in silence.

"I loved beauty shop days." Annie pushed her wispy bangs out of her face. "Remember those? We should do that now, a makeover night with your mom's dresses."

"Totally." I beamed. Maybe subbing had done more for me than I'd realized. One little shoulder poke and I was back in. And maybe Celeste would finally get over it and move on!

"That would rock!" Celeste stepped forward, suddenly animated.

Annie's and Nikki's eyes lit up, relieved by her approval.

"Let's do a slumber party and tell more stories from the good old days." Celeste lowered her voice. "Here's one."

We leaned in. She always did know how to tell a story.

"Remember when Desi's perfect mom and happy little family weren't enough for her do-gooder dad? So he had to find more ways to show his awesomeness by sending my dad to prison and ruining my life? And Desi didn't even try to stop it, not once, just let it happen?" Her small body shook. "Anyone else remember *that*?"

Celeste let out a sob and ran out of the tent. I turned to Annie and Nikki, silently begging them, *pleading* for them not to rush after her, to consider my side of the mess, what my social life had been like over the last two years.

Annie looked up. Nikki looked down. The HMs shuffled out of the tent in one uniform, camisoled line. And I was left alone.

Again.

I drifted out of the food tent, only managing to take a few directionless steps before Drake ran up to me. "Dude, there you are! Come on. I need your help at our booth."

I followed him, Idaho-dazed, not sure or caring where he was leading me. Laughter burst from every booth we passed, every corner. Two little girls huddled under a picnic table, sharing cotton candy.

Acceptance. It was so close, sweeter than any blue-ribbon pie. Celeste had snatched it away again. Why couldn't I change their minds? What did it take? I felt so completely powerless, like I was melting right into the dirt floor.

Drake stopped.

I stopped.

He pointed. "Do you want a suit or anything?"

I squinted in the sunlight. We were at the end of the carnival booths, next to the milk toss. A yellow rusted dunk tank filled with swirling water bore a poster board with the Pets Charming logo and the invitation: "Watch us swim with the fish! Three tickets." A blue tarp formed a wall that stretched down over the grass. The softball-size target jutted out about chest level from the tarp.

A line of tormenters had already formed.

"I'm supposed to get in there?" I asked, panicked. Leave it to Pets Charming to up the humiliation ante.

"Yeah well, you said you'd work at our booth. And . . . uh, this is our booth."

I didn't move.

Drake fidgeted. "We're out of volunteers. I'd get in myself but I have to take tickets and, well, I, uh . . . have a rash. Look, do this for me and I'll make the groundhog costume up to you. I promise."

The sunlight glinted off the water, hypnotizing me. "Yeah. You better."

I climbed the four slick steps like a princess ascending her tower, and perched myself on the wet seat, hairs prickling out of the goose bumps covering my legs. My body kept functioning, my heart kept beating, my lungs kept breathing, but I wasn't there anymore. I was in the big Idaho sky, watching the poor girl who flinched every time someone threw a softball and missed the target.

Fortunately, no one athletically inclined seemed interested in the dunking game. Ball after ball whizzed past, and not one hit the target. My shoulders relaxed. I still might come out of this with a shred of dignity.

"Okay, Desi." Drake tapped the tank. "Just a few more and you're free."

Free. I sent up a quick prayer of thanks to God or the tree spirits or the MP goddess. Whoever or whatever it was that had kept me mostly dry.

And then I saw Hayden through the hazy fiberglass, stretching his biceps. The HMs and Celeste were ominously gathered around him.

Ta-ta, dignity.

Hayden waved at me. "Ready for a dip?" he called.

"Not really!" Surely he would hear the desperation in my voice and drop the ball. Or even better, climb into the tank with me, wrap his fingers into mine, and say, "I'm back, Desi. Your Boggle Boy is back."

He spit into his hands, rubbed them together, then fingered the ball. "Prepare to meet your doom!"

For someone as cool as Hayden, "Prepare to meet your

doom" was a lame line. It sounded like something roly-poly Romeo from the Mutant Insect Battalion would say, not something coming out of the mouth of a worthy crush. And shouldn't someone worth crushing on detect my fear? Wouldn't he want to keep me dry and cute, not banish me to the aquatic abyss?

I wiggled my toes, suddenly aware of where they were. I'd soon be soaked, my hair would frizz, and I don't think Mom had used waterproof mascara. Even worse, Celeste was there, savoring my humiliation. Hayden wound up his arm and released the softball. It catapulted in slow motion until it nicked the side of the target. I squeezed my eyes shut, waiting for the splash.

It didn't come. I pried one eye open.

Hayden rubbed his chiseled jaw. "Is your tank broken?" he asked Drake.

Someone giggled.

Before Drake could answer, Celeste broke free and tapped her fingernails on the front of the fiberglass, a sound that made chalkboard scratching seem melodic. "I can fix it," she said.

My voice caught in my throat. It was like when I'd first seen Lord of Pray: I couldn't get a sound out. Couldn't scream at her to stop.

She placed one hand on the red target and used the other to blow me a kiss. The look on her face was cruel, of course, but also kind of weird. Like . . . jealous. I was the one in the dunk tank, and she had my crush. And my friends. What did she have to be jealous about?

The seat collapsed and I plunged into the silver water.

I've heard it said that when you drown, there is a moment of clarity right before you black out. There's peace and tranquility in letting go of the fight, letting the element overtake you. And even though I was only drowning in humiliation, things were still pretty clear.

Something small had solidified within me, and it went beyond tiaras and princess puff. My impact muscle had grown both times I'd landed in those different cultures, plunged into those girls' lives and situations, and squeezed their need for something more, something greater, out of them. It wasn't what I'd asked for, but it was what I'd gotten.

And I wanted more and more and more.

There wasn't a fish or anything else organic nearby to link my MP with, so I went as Zen as I could, fiercely wishing for Meredith to appear.

Ohhmmmmm. Ohmmmm. Was this how it worked? Perhaps it would help if I knew what Zen actually meant. So I did it the old-fashioned way. "MEREDITH! HELP!" I choked on my scream, water filling my lungs.

A bubble formed in the water, shimmery and small. I could just make out Meredith's outline in it, mouthing something. Paddling closer, I heard her faint demand.

"Grab it!" she said.

The bubble popped in my hands. My body was sucked in, out of the water, out of Sproutville. I collided with a black hardwood floor, coughing, water splashing around me.

A green stiletto tapped below my dripping chin. "Darling, you really need to enroll in a swim class."

I coughed again. Meredith flung a black waffle-weaved towel at me. I buried my face in it and tried to stop shaking.

"So, you rang?" She unbuttoned her white peacoat, tossed it onto her office chair, and retied the already perfect bow of her green wrap dress. Her hands settled on her hips, one foot out in her signature Meredith pose.

"I guess you could call it that." I hugged my knees, my brown skirt clinging to my legs. "Look, I don't know what you've decided but . . . up until the bubble incident, I was doing a good job, Meredith. And I'm really, really sorry, and you were really, really right, and I was very, very wrong. So what if you brought me back? Let me prove myself. I'll be the impersonation queen. Well, princess. Even *you* won't know the difference."

Meredith retrieved another towel from the bathroom and primly kneeled to blot her waxed floor. "That's it? I was hoping for some more begging. At least flattery."

"Um . . . I like your dress?"

"Of course you do. It cost more than your entire T-shirt collection." Meredith chucked the towel at me, and I took it as my cue to clean up the rest of the water. "Here's the thing. From what I've seen, I don't know how the princesses could possibly be happy with the stunts you've pulled."

"Why wouldn't they be? I *helped* them, Meredith. And how are they doing? I wonder if Simmy's French horn is fixed. Or if Ama wound up with that guy. I wish I could talk to them and see what they think."

"Well, we aren't certain what they think at the moment, because Central Command still hasn't cleared up the PPR issue." She cocked her head to the side. "If your performance was really poor, though, the princesses would have probably contacted us in person. So that's hopeful. But, since it's you, I could also assume they're just too busy cleaning up your disasters and haven't had time. We'll see."

I stopped mopping. "All I heard was the word *hopeful*."

"The truth is," Meredith went on, "we're in a wholly unique situation, and all you've botched on *paper* was the emergency bubble, and there's a chance that might even stay off record. And by the way, the bubble was fixed, but I'm going to have to dock your pay from the previous gigs to cover the repairs and cover your butt."

"Anything," I pleaded.

"So, I have this assignment. BUT"—she closed her eyes and shook her head—"you *have* to understand this is a once-in-a-lifetime opportunity you don't even deserve. Princess Elsa is technically a Level One, but there's likelihood she'll become a Level Three; she certainly has the pedigree. She's leaving for a couple of days and has never had a sub before, and a princess's first sub—if she does well—has a big advantage when the princess is auditioning for a Match. Desi, this is a big deal."

"Wow. And you trust me with this? Thank you."

Meredith snorted. "Trust you? This could very well be the biggest mistake of my career!"

Wounded, I hung the towels back on the rack. I needed to let her insults roll off me. Regardless of what she said, I had to be good enough or she wouldn't be letting me do this.

Meredith was back at her desk when I came in, and we, it appeared, were back in business.

"So, as you've heard, Lady Carol is getting married this weekend, and every royal from here to Antarctica is invited. It's bound to be spectacular, but half of the guest list is snatching up subs, leaving poor Level One Elsa stuck."

I knew it. "So you're taking me back because you're shorthanded."

"I could put you back in that dunk—Ow!" Meredith frantically grabbed at her pocket. "Stupid zapping mail alerts." She tossed me my manual. "Read it. And here's your rouge."

Swallowing my smile, I clicked on the message and applied some rouge. The princess's picture dazzled, while the profile info underwhelmed.

Princess Elsa of the House of Holdenzastein

Age: 15

Hometown: Metzahg. Small village in the eastern Alps.

Favorite Color: Blue

Favorite Food: Anything not microwaved. And Nana Helga's stroganoff, but only if she's in a good mood when she makes it. Otherwise, you never know what'll end up in there.

Favorite Book: *The Princess Diaries* by Meg Cabot

Family Information: My mom died over a year ago, I never met my dad, and I'm an only child. I live with Nana Helga. Princess Helga of the Imperial and Royal House of Holdenzastein, actually, but she'll punch you if you call her that. If there were words to describe her, I would, but there aren't. She means well. Oh, and remind her to take her heart meds!!!

Cultural Traditions: Culture? That's a good one. My mom used to take me to concerts and lectures whenever she could, but now I'm pretty secluded from all of that. I miss it. All of it.

Anything Else We Should Know: I don't like nuts. My hair needs to be brushed twice a day or it gets knots. I like things in order. . . .

Look. My life is pretty boring. Your other jobs are probably tons better. I just really need a break to clear my head.

I stared at her picture. Elsa was the kind of doe-eyed, hourglass-shaped girl who inspired cartoonists' princesses. How could a girl like her be so obviously depressed?

"You guys seriously have to work on these profiles! This one is shorter than Simmy's."

"I imagine she really is bored out of her mind. Elsa's known as 'the lost princess.' The country her great-great-grandfather ruled was broken up after the First World War. The family . . ." Meredith leaned toward her computer screen and read: "The House of Hol-den-*za*-stein, gets to keep their title even without a country, and there's still plenty of family cash and castles and other royal bling. But Elsa's eccentric grandmother withdrew from society and refuses to access any of the wealth, which is too bad because Elsa really has some potential. Elsa's mother gave her a proper education and upbringing, despite their lack of money, before she died of cancer. But now Elsa lives with her Nana Helga in a tiny cottage in the Alps."

"That's dumb. Why would anyone give up being a royal?"

Meredith's screen saver flashed on, a picture of a dark brick tunnel, with small pinprick of white in the middle. Meredith sighed. "There are valid reasons."

"Name three."

"Balance. Desire for privacy. And sometimes . . . love." The bubble shook and Meredith looked away. "The longer you do this, Desi, the more confusing it all becomes."

I remembered Lilith's accidental mention of a scandal, and wondered what confusion Meredith had experienced, what tunnels she'd stumbled through in her own sub wanderings. Her stare was so blank, I doubted she was actually seeing anything in the room at the moment. Perhaps I should offer a hug. Or some psychological advice. "Meredith, look, we never really talk about stuff—"

Meredith snapped her head down and flicked her fingers across her keyboard, Mozart-style. "We've been here for a minute already, and you're about two away from changing."

"I know, but maybe it'd be good for our relationship—"

She stood and pointed at the bubble wall. "Worry less about me and more about your job. And if you have an emergency the manual can't explain, my e-mail is in your address book. But don't get caught! Now, shoo! My gosh! It's like talking to a drunk duke or something."

"Fine. I'm leaving." I burst through the bubble, which was still hovering a few feet above the ground. A mound of horse manure softened my fall.

Not a very royal entrance.

Chapter 16

*L*uckily, no one saw my arrival. No one except the chipper animals frolicking in the meadow. That's right— little squirrels chattering in harmony with bees buzzing and songbirds singing. And the meadow blanketed a sloping hill in purple and yellow wildflowers for miles and miles. Funny I would land in a pile of manure in the middle of such perfection. Meredith must have planned a little welcome-back present. At least my hands were clean.

But it was hard to stay mad when there was fresh sunshine beating down on my mountain maiden face. I stood there for a moment enjoying the warmth while I transformed into Elsa. My hair formed into golden blond braids, my clothes into khaki shorts and a simple blue top. I felt my face, knowing without seeing that I/Elsa was beautiful.

When I was completely Elsa-ized, I had the giddy desire to sing *The Sound of Music* song about the hills being alive and my heart being . . . Oh man, I couldn't remember the words. My heart dances like the wind? No, um, sings like a . . . songbird?

Anyway, here I was, probably in the same spot they'd filmed that movie. I threw back my head, raised my arms, and allowed the inner Julie Andrews in me to explode.

Thirty dizzying seconds later, the hills *were* alive with the sound of music. Well, not really music. I'm a pretty good singer, but Elsa was close to tone-deaf.

"Ach! Did you swallow a swallow? What's that horrible sound?"

A woman with poofy dyed red hair and lipstick to match frowned up at me. She picked her way up the hill in fuzzy lime flip-flops and a floral print blouse that blew in the Alpine breeze, blending into the landscape about as well as Meredith would in Idaho.

"Oh!" I flopped to the ground. Elsa's profile info did not quite do Nana Helga justice.

"What's with the dancing?" she asked.

"Twirling. I thought I was alone."

Nana Helga sniffed the air. "Smells like you were twirling in horse manure. Go shower. I need to get down to the village so we can pick up my heart pills."

We headed down the hill toward what I could only guess was my home for however long Meredith had sent me here.

The porch sagged, and one of the window shutters hung from a hinge. It took my eyes a bit to adjust once I'd ducked inside. The living room was filled with antiques—not fancy royal antiques, just furniture that had never been replaced. And there wasn't much of it, much of anything. It was as if Nana Helga had removed anything that might pass for royal in her pursuit to shun her past.

Great. I bet I wouldn't even have a hair dryer here.

"Well, what are you waiting for?" Nana Helga nudged me toward the stairs. "My heart's going to stop if we don't leave soon. You smell like a cow. Go wash up."

Elsa's bathroom was right at the top of the stairs. Chipped tile and cracked plaster, Victorian-style fixtures, with an oval-shaped mirror hanging over a tiny porcelain sink. I showered and toweled off quickly, then carefully rebraided Elsa's long blond hair.

The face looking back at me in the mirror seemed to belong in a fairy tale book: delicate and glowing without any makeup. And I know this doesn't make sense, because it was me inside of there, but somehow I could tell that Elsa was sad. I felt her sadness—in a way it belonged to me too. She had circles under her eyes and tiny worry lines in her forehead. This was a girl who needed some impact. But why? And how?

I got my first clue when I came back downstairs. Nana Helga, who clearly was color-blind, wore mismatched shoes—the left one, road-sign orange; the right, green with tiny flowers. I had no idea if Elsa would point something like this out but . . . who wouldn't? It was so *wrong*.

"Nana, are you sure you want to wear those shoes?" I asked carefully.

Nana Helga squinted down at her feet then broke into a nutty cackle. "Don't you like my look? Haven't you heard? This is all the rage in Paris!"

I bit my lip. She didn't need to be rude. I was just trying to help.

"Quick, call the paparazzi! Post it in your *Royalty News* magazine. Another royal has made a fashion faux pas. The world will come to an end. Civilizations will crumble! Please, Elsa. Maybe I *like* to wear mismatched shoes. Proves how little I care about all those elitist buffoons."

I tried not to look stunned. Elsa was probably used to such outbursts. Poor girl. "Sorry."

On the way out, I grabbed a gardening magazine from the three-legged coffee table (not the top of it. The fourth leg *was* a stack of magazines) so I could pretend to read it and hopefully disguise the fact that I had no idea where we were going. Nana Helga hobbled ahead of me, muttering to herself under her breath.

The more time I spent with Nana Helga, the clearer it became that she and Elsa were not in the habit of holding hands and enjoying quality time together. More than anything, Helga seemed determined to annoy and embarrass her granddaughter as much as possible.

Although the magazine helped minimize conversation with Nana Helga (and taught me the best time to plant daffodil bulbs), it kept me from taking in the full beauty of the village. I tried to stay focused and not stare at the rustic storefronts and quaint farmers' market, all things Elsa would be wholly familiar with and so uninterested in exploring.

As soon as we walked into the village pharmacy, Nana waddled straight to the counter at the back. "Hey, Edgar, those pills won't pour themselves."

I left the two of them to chat and browsed a chocolate aisle the size of Hershey, Pennsylvania.

Almonds or no almonds? Truffles? Hazelnuts? Oh, wait. Elsa doesn't like nuts. At least she didn't have braces. Bingo. Caramel.

I automatically dug into my pockets. Great. Of course I was subbing for the penniless princess when I finally beheld European chocolate Nirvana. Sighing, I put the sweet bar of goodness back on the shelf.

"How much do you need?" asked a male, accented voice.

I whirled around. In front of me was Prince Karl of Fenmar. THE Prince Karl, the younger brother of the hottest man alive, Prince Barrett. Here. In Elsa's village. Staring at my frozen hand and smiling tentatively.

"Well? How much?"

"I . . . I . . . Three . . . three . . . euros? But it's fine. Don't worry about it."

He held out the money, his gold cuff links catching the light. "No, really. It's the least I can do for an old friend. Come now, Elsa. Aren't you going to say hello?"

Of all the awkward subbing moments, figuring out how

Elsa knew Prince Karl and how *well* she knew him was the worst. Well, after dancing half naked. And, okay, the roly-poly incident.

I took the money out of his still-outstretched hand and smiled. "Thanks. Uh . . . it's good to see you. How . . . are you?"

"Brilliant. I saw you across the village square and thought I'd stop in and say hello." Prince Karl cast his dark eyes around the store. "This whole village is a massive mob."

I looked around the store. It was nearly empty, but there was a huge crowd gathered outside the window, watching us. "I know. What's with that? You'd swear they've never seen two people buying a candy bar before."

He nodded eagerly. "Good form, Elsa. Yes. Yes, just buying a candy, eh?"

I finally lowered my hand and shifted my weight, unsure if I'd made a wrong move. Was Elsa funny? Did Karl know her well enough to know her sense of humor? Was he teasing? Aside from Drake, I didn't know any older guys.

"Listen, I'm here on holiday for a few days, and I'd really like for us to sit down and talk." He scanned the store, looking for a seat. "Or not sit down."

"No, it's fine. We can stand, Your Highness."

He startled. "Elsa, since when do you call me Your Highness?"

Uh-oh. Ugh! Why wasn't there anything about this prince in Elsa's bio? "Since . . . now?"

"Just Karl is fine."

"Okay . . . Karl. What did you need to talk to me about?"

"Oh." Karl ran a hand down his face. "Well, first off, how is everything? How is . . . your Nana Helga?"

We glanced at Nana Helga, who glowered back at us. "Friendly as ever," I said.

"Yes. Quite right. And you? Have you been well? I'm sorry I haven't . . . called. There are things I've wanted to say that I felt you deserved to hear in person."

"Yes?" I asked.

"Yes?"

"What did you want to say?"

"Oh . . . um . . . well, let me just tell you I think you are wonderful. You know that, right? You're an incredible friend and probably the sweetest girl I've met. Ever."

So did they like each other? Was he asking her out, here? Or was he giving her the "friends" line because they used to be an item? Was this a breakup? I needed to get away and check the manual! "Thank you. That's very kind."

Karl was gazing at me. Taking in every line on Elsa's face, like a silent movie actor who can't say how he feels, and has to show it with his eyes. "Elsa, it's always shocking to see how . . . You look nice."

I looked down, uncomfortable. "Thanks. So was that it?"

He reached a hand out like he was going to touch me, and grabbed two caramel bars instead. "No. It's not. Maybe this isn't the best setting. I'd love for you to come visit our summer home."

Come on, MP. Give me a clue what's going on here. "Wow, um . . ."

"It's only Barrett and me. Mother and Father didn't want him attending the wedding after his last escapade, so we came here last minute. Well, I've been hoping to come anyway, so this worked out. I'm my brother's keeper, I suppose." He smiled at the floor. "Perhaps you can help me."

My eyes nearly popped out. ME! MEET PRINCE BARRETT!!!!! Whoa, whoa . . . and whoa. If I see Prince Barrett, I might have a heart attack. Or a heat stroke from all his hotness. I tried to contain my excitement. "That would be great!"

Prince Karl frowned in concentration. "When would be an appropriate time? I could send a car or something."

Let's see. Busy schedule back at the Casa AntiRoyal. "I can make time for you."

"See? So sweet." Prince Karl stared at me again, his expression edging on anguished, before turning away, suddenly hurried. "I can't tell you how relieved I am that we can finally talk. It's been a long time coming."

I followed him to the counter and handed his money to the openmouthed cashier.

"Thank you again," I said.

"You're welcome." Karl did a quick little bow. "Enjoy your chocolate, Elsa. I'll call you soon."

He walked out of the store and into a mob of villagers, which swallowed all five and a half feet of him in seconds. Men in black suits swept in and ushered him into a limousine.

As the limo drove away, Nana Helga stormed up next to me. "Please tell me you didn't just agree to see the Prince of Fenmar again."

"I guess I just did."

"Humph. You know how I feel about *those* people." She folded her strong arms across her chest. "*Schatz*, I know you two were friends when you were kids, but you're a big girl now. So why don't you run out there and tell that boy to shove off?"

Whew-hoo-hoo. Issues, much? I doubted Elsa had any say when it came to "those people." I surveyed Nana Helga. When you're facing a hard wall, a few rocks aren't going to shake it down. So instead of fighting it, I tried to find a way around. "Maybe you're right."

"I'm glad you finally get it. Your mother never did."

I unwrapped the chocolate and took a delicious bite, but the sweetness couldn't counteract Nana Helga's bitterness. Looked like I'd have to go stealth on this job.

Chapter 17

When we got back, Nana Helga tore open the frost-filled freezer and slapped two frozen dinners on the counter. "Cook these in the oven this time; it tastes better. And bring them into the TV room when they're done." Her polyester pants brushed together as she shuffled out of the room.

Yuck. Half-dark, half-white turkey meat. All natural, sodium free. I stuck them into the easy-bake-looking oven and poked around the kitchen for some real food. Goat cheese, apples, and old bread. Royal, if you're living in the 1300s.

While "dinner" cooked, I ran upstairs to Elsa's room. I'd learned from my Simmy experience that you could find out more about a person just snooping around than you could from those stupid profiles.

There wasn't much to investigate. Elsa's wardrobe was monochromatic—T-shirts and button-downs, all blue, white, or gray. Khakis in every color. One white floor-length dress with a matching jacket that probably hadn't fit Elsa in years languished in the farthest corner of her closet. I fingered the stiff fabric, imagining what royal engagements, if any, Elsa had attended.

I bumped into her nicked dresser and heard a tinkling from inside the second drawer. Underneath a stack of neatly tucked white socks was a silver jewelry box, the kind locked behind glass doors in nice antique stores. A remnant of the royal days. But the real treasures were inside: pictures of Elsa with her mom, who was every bit as beautiful as her daughter; a fraying luncheon invitation dated five years back, bearing Prince Karl's family crest; sapphire stud earrings and a silver oval-shaped locket. Eager for a clue, I carefully opened the oval, but it was empty.

I set the box and necklace on the dresser. Elsa's privacy had officially been invaded already, so I thought I might as well go for the gold. I dropped down to my hands and knees and fumbled under her bed until I found an unassuming spiral notebook with I ♥ KARL scrawled in flowing print on the cover.

Newspaper cutouts about Karl and his family were pasted onto the pages, along with dried flowers and photographs of Elsa and Karl from childhood to their early teens. There were also drawings of Karl's hands, his family crest, and a tree swing with "Our tree" written underneath.

The sweetest things were the notes. They started off simple, the *Do you like me? Check yes or no* variety, but over the years, Karl and Elsa had written more—shared more in their letters. The most recent was dated over a year ago. Karl had even written—get this—*poetry* for Elsa. The last poem read:

Those golden braids
Are just like you
So complex, yet so simple
Beautiful and steady
They're also like us
Me and you
Parts divided, overlapping
But that third piece
It surrounds us
Keeps us apart
If we can cut it
Then it will just be
Me and you
Forever

Then there were a few months of nothing—no pictures or letters. Finally, Elsa started keeping journal-style notes, beginning a few months back.

Today I was in the antique store with
Nana Helga and saw these old gold cuff links

with an engraved tree. They were so Karl, I
didn't care that they cost me nearly all of
my savings (which was only about thirty euros,
but anyway). Nana would kill me if she
knew, but I sent them to Karl with a little
"Thinking of you" note. And I wrote _love_ at
the end. Not I love you. Just love. That's
okay, right?

A week later:

Was that stalkerlike of me to send those
cuff links? We haven't talked in forever,
but that never mattered before. And I know
he likely has a million pairs of cuff links,
but . . . it's the thought that counts, isn't
it? Anyway, I just haven't heard from him.
I'd hoped it would be a good reconnection
of sorts. Maybe he threw away the envelope
and doesn't have my return address? Or
the palace mail carrier hasn't delivered
them yet?

Another week later:

Still nothing. I know he was at an event
for Africa Is Hungry last weekend, so maybe
he's busy. I love that about him—he's always

contributing to all these causes and he's so passionate about them! I wish I could be a part of it. I even mentioned to Nana how much I'd like to help out. When she made fun of charities, I tried to think of something smaller, something local, like starting a new soup kitchen. At this point, I'd be happy to attend a charity polo match! Anything to get out of the house! But Nana Helga shouted a big N-O. It's such a waste that I just sit here in this house. If I was real royalty, not whatever-I-am-now, I would really change things, you know? I want to matter.

A month later:

I heard from my old friend Petrina. She said she'd heard a rumor at her school about Karl and some girl. And if it's true then I guess that explains why I never heard back from him. My heart . . . it's breaking. It's broken.

My heart broke *for* her. Maybe because I kind of . . . *was* her. I could totally see us being friends. Just like me, she wanted something bigger. And she had liked a guy—Prince Karl—forever. Pretty much a royal version of my Hayden thing, except there was no evidence of a dunk-tank disaster in her book.

There weren't any posts about Elsa on the message board, so I put in an inquiry on the General Quick Tips thread.

LostLoveFound?: Hey, apparently Elsa is friends with Prince Karl and there is a rumor swirling around about another girl. Any hints who she is? Because three's a crowd, if you know what I mean!

My answer came quickly.

ALittleBird: There's all sorts of stuff on the Karl thread. Check out this link and here's a pic that might help. Who is Elsa anyway? Some Level One?

The picture—grainy and taken from far away, no doubt by a paparazzo—showed Karl on a yacht in those yucky boxer-brief swim trunks, lying next to a bikini-clad girl with a towel covering her face.

I clicked on the Karl link to figure out who the girl was.

SinkMySub34: The girl in the Karl picture is definitely Duchess Olivia. She's actually a sweet gig if you can get it—sunbathing on a yacht all day in the Mediterranean, wearing dental-floss bikinis. So question: are they dating?

LetThemEatCake: Yep. I can tell you firsthand Olivia is dating Prince Karl and has an interview coming out where she confirms it. I think it's mostly an image thing, but she wants her subs playing it up big-time now. I mean, wear an I ♥ PRINCE KARL! shirt big-time. And can you believe her bikinis?

Ah, so . . . all that "you're the sweetest girl" and "I wanted to do this in person" stuff was Karl trying to tell me about the Duchess of Dental Floss. And if Elsa knew the whole story, oh man. She would be even more crushed.

Meredith said to contact her with an emergency. Yeah well, there was no way the manual covered *love triangles*! I sent her a short e-mail:

> Meredith,
> I need your help. This prince just popped into town. I'm not sure what his intentions are, but Elsa's known him forever. She's in love with him, but he has a girlfriend. . . . What should I do?
> —Desi

Within moments of sending, a message pinged in my inbox.

MAIL DELIVERY FAILURE: Princess mail temporarily unavailable. Your message cannot be sent.

Well, I guess my choice was made for me. I couldn't let

Elsa down; I'd just figured out how to impact. Sorry, Princey. You aren't getting rid of these golden braids that easily.

Prince Karl's thin nose and close-cropped brown hair flashed in my mind. It'd be nice if he were at least cute. Or Prince Barrett. But whatever. He didn't really have anything to do with me. This was all Elsa. Get Prince Charming for the lost princess and get out.

Easy peasy.

Chapter 18

The brunch invite came the next morning via a footman. Okay, maybe he wasn't a footman. A royal worker of some sort. But footman sounds so cool, right? Almost as cool as being invited to brunch. And, seriously, this had to mean Karl felt something for Elsa. I'd seen the way he looked at her. And they had so much *history*.

Unless this brunch was just a private place for him to give her the royal boot. In which case, I would be all charms, all sweetness. Not to mention I planned on putting Elsa's classic beauty to good use. I realized love issues might be one of the hardest ways to impact, because there's only so much you can control, but it was a fight any screen siren would gallantly take on. I would channel my inner Grace Kelly. No guy could resist that.

My plan was quickly nixed when Nana Helga snuck up on me and read the invitation.

"What is THAT?"

I hid the paper behind my back. "What?"

"This." She grabbed the paper and held it up between her purple polished nails.

"Um, an invitation. To brunch. Really quality paper, huh?"

Nana Helga ripped the paper in half and tossed it on the coffee table.

I folded my arms. Whoa, okay, so Nana needed some impacting of her own. This whole forcing-Elsa-not-to-be-royal thing was not jiving with me. Why deprive her grand-daughter of all those opportunities just because she's some bitter grump? Elsa had mentioned a polo match. At the very least I would get that girl to a polo match.

"Nana. Come on."

"Either that boy is persistent, or you didn't give him the brush-off."

"I know. But we're friends." I picked up the shreds of paper so I could save it for Elsa's Karl book. "We've been friends for a long time."

"You're not going."

"Please? Please, you never let me do anything. And you don't know how long I've been waiting for something exciting like this! And Karl's very . . ." I grasped for a word. Serious? Brooding? Awkward? "Polite. It's not like I'm asking to go to a gala. It's just brunch. *Please?*"

"We are not even discussing this." Her face and hair meshed together into one mad flame. "Go to your room."

I stormed upstairs and slammed the door behind me. This was so unfair to Elsa. Plus, I'd been waiting for a sub adventure like this since I'd signed on the magical line. I couldn't impact while sitting in this stupid bedroom in this tiny house.

No crotchety grandma was going to stop me.

I raked through Elsa's wardrobe. Let's see, I could wear a blue shirt with khakis. Or a gray shirt with khakis. Or a gray-ish blue shirt . . . with khakis. There was that white dress suit, but no way would that work. Unless . . .

I yanked it out of the closet and held it up to Elsa in the mirror. Maybe it wasn't as old as I thought. The jacket, shoulder pads and all, had to go, but the sheath dress was decent. I slid it over my head. Whoa, I/she/we actually looked pretty hot. All I needed to do was hem it, and it'd be the perfect white summer dress. Easy enough. I paired it with some simple sandals and Nana's antique yellow shawl that was straight vintage glamour. It matched Elsa's blond hair, which I could let out of its braids and . . . Ooh! Elsa had those gorgeous sapphire earrings and locket. . . .

I beamed at Elsa in the mirror. I could do this. Forget the evil Nana; Elsarella was totally going to the ball.

Five minutes before eleven, I stepped into the kitchen. Nana Helga's head was bent over a large pot of cabbage soup.

Closing her eyes, she took a taste from the cracked wooden spoon and nodded.

I tiptoed past her toward the door.

"Elsa. Don't."

I spun around slowly. "I have to go."

"I thought you were smarter than this."

"I'm going to brunch with a prince, Nana Helga. It's a total no-brainer."

Finally, Helga turned around. Her face softened when she saw me. "Is that the dress you wore to the symphony with your mother and me? Vivaldi. She loved Vivaldi." She swallowed. "And those earrings . . . I thought you'd stopped wearing those to spite me."

I tugged at my earlobe. "I love these earrings."

"They're one of the only things I kept from my grand-mother. I always thought they matched your eyes."

"Thank you."

"Well, they never did much for me." She went back to stirring her soup. "If you leave this house, you'll regret it. Truly."

"I'll regret it more if I don't." I walked purposefully out the front door before Nana Helga could say anything else. Surprised she didn't follow me, I clicked the door shut. Well, she hadn't locked me in a tower. That had to be progress.

Karl said he'd send a "car or something," but he'd obviously used that term very loosely because there was actually a limo parked just outside the house. No "something" about it. One of his bodyguards stepped out and opened my door for me.

"My lady," he said.

I dipped into an awkward curtsy before sliding into the car.

Which had a flat screen.

And a bar.

And room for twenty.

I folded my hands in my lap, determined not to explore the interior wonders. That's what a common girl would do. Actually, they'd probably open the sunroof to behold the Alps while lounging on the leather (massaging!) seats.

I wasn't going to be the OH-MY-GOSH-I'VE-NEVER-BEEN-IN-A-LIMO girl.

Oh, and surround-sound speakers.

It was the longest car ride of my life.

I should have known, of course, that "summer house" really translated to *Pride and Prejudice*–style MANOR complete with a mile-long front lawn and a stone nymph fountain. I was so focused on looking like I belonged that I didn't get intimidated until we walked into the front entryway.

The driver led me in and introduced me to a butler, who took my shawl and hung it in a closet underneath the left staircase. (Yeah, left. Meaning there was a *right* staircase, both with slide-worthy banisters.) Life-size portraits of Karl and his family—father, mother, and older brother—hung where the staircases split. Karl looked like he was posing for an outdated JCPenney catalog. Seriously, I bet if you turned to the school uniform section, he'd be there, hair combed to the side and every crease annoyingly pressed.

Barrett, on the other hand, somehow managed to look cool and gorgeous in his military uniform. And I was maybe going to meet him!

Stay focused, Desi. You're here to impact, which means being as charming as possible so Karl will be smitten once again and Elsa can come home to her lost love.

My escort led me down the wide hallway, portraits of dead royals following us as we walked. "His Highness is in the entertainment room." He motioned toward a closed door. "Brunch will be served shortly."

I gingerly placed my fingers on the doorknob. Wait, wasn't I supposed to be announced?

I didn't have to press my ear against the door to hear the voices. There had to be five people behind there, and they were all shouting. Violently.

Was the family fighting over my invite? Maybe Nana Helga was right. I was way out of my league and I should just . . .

Stop it.

It's brunch.

Brunch with a high-school-aged prince who thought I was an older and wiser sort-of princess.

I shook the handle as a warning before turning it slowly. When the door opened, the sound was amplified by a few thousand decibels. Rock music.

The room was not filled with a mass of royals shouting at each other. Actually, it wasn't filled with anything. One mile-long couch wrapped around the room. Some skateboarding video game lit up a screen worthy of a small movie theater. Karl swerved along with his controller.

"Get it! No! Come on. Get in there!" he yelled.

I stood there, unnoticed, and took in Karl's appearance. His usually perfectly parted hair looked slightly tousled. Half of his oxford shirt was untucked. And he was smiling, smiling wide, like playing this game was the most fun he'd ever had. I inched farther into the room until I was standing next to him.

"Elsa." Karl dropped his remote. "I didn't hear you."

"Don't stop," I said, pointing. "You're about to"—the screen filled with red—"crash."

Karl meandered around the couch and flipped on a light switch. "I didn't realize it was time for brunch already. I'm so sorry." He frantically smoothed his hair, but missed one giant cowlick.

"It's fine. So . . . ?"

"Right, brunch! Come on." Karl stiffly offered his elbow and led me to a small, cozy garden room. He pulled out my chair for me before easing into his own seat. He cleared his throat and said, "You look very comely, Elsa."

Comely? Gosh, he was such a dork, even if he looked a little better all ruffled and untucked. But it was still a compliment—one point for Elsa. I flashed a smile. "Thank you, Karl. You look handsome. You always do."

"Oh, thanks. You should have seen me this morning, though. Hives. And I'm pretty concerned about this skin fungus I seem to have developed."

"Uh, skin fungus?"

Karl stuck his foot on his chair and started to roll up his pant leg. "You want me to show you? It doesn't flare up so much in this climate, but it's still rather disgus—"

"That's okay. Why don't you . . . tell me about school instead?"

"School? Oh." Karl knit his eyebrows together. "Well, I studied quite a bit in school. Fascinating things, like . . . Greek philosophy. Yeah. Philosophy."

Philosophy? I kept my face taut, swallowing a mammoth yawn.

"Would you like to hear about Aristotle's theory of universals?" Karl added. "I could talk for hours—"

"Actually, I'd much rather talk about, um, *your* life. What have you been up to?"

Karl squirmed. "Well. Hey, do you like hunting?"

"*Hunting?*" What was up with this guy? "Not really."

"Oh, well, I do. Every day, I . . . hunt. Shoot loads of animals. Loads."

Don't get weirded out, Desi. This is for Elsa. Stick to your mission—reminding him how wonderful Elsa is. I flipped her beautiful blond hair and batted her long eyelashes. "I hope I dressed all right for brunch," I said coyly.

"Sure." Karl scratched his leg. "Hey, am I bothering you at all?"

Yes. "No. Not at all! I'm having a lovely time."

"Oh." He slumped back in his chair. "Splendid."

Wait, did he *want* to bother me? Holy hunting. He was being lame on purpose so she wouldn't be interested! Well sorry, buddy. I read that little poem you wrote. This is for your benefit too. I'm not giving up yet.

We both looked around the room, at everything but each other. I'd underestimated Karl and the situation. I racked my brain for . . . anything. A connection. Something he cared about. I drew in a long breath. "So. Tell me about the work you've done in Africa lately."

"Oh! Well, we're trying to provide goats for families right now. Goats can transform a village—there's the milk, not to mention the fertilizer from manure. . . ." Karl looked down. "You probably don't want to hear about all this."

"No, I think it's fascinating," I said. Manure for charities was still better than discussing a royal fungus. "If Nana Helga would actually let me out of the house, I'd love to be out there, raising awareness."

"At a fancy event, right? So you could wear a dress."

"It's not about that! I mean, sure, I'd love to go to an event. Go anywhere outside of Nana Helga's, but I don't know. Helping people who have nothing makes me realize I have more than I thought. You know?"

Karl didn't say anything, but I definitely had his attention.

"This goat idea," I continued, "it reminds me of that

179

saying—something about, you give a man a fish and it feeds him for a day—"

"But teach him to fish and it feeds him for life. Yes! That's like farming, you know. Teach farmers how to minimize soil erosion and rotate crops, and—"

"And you've solved a continuing problem—"

"Exactly! Education *and* resources is the key." Karl shook his head and stared at me. "Huh . . . This isn't what I expected."

What had he expected? That he'd just ride his horse into town, kick Elsa away, and polish off his boot when he was done?

I was hanging on with just my instincts here. He flipped moods so much my MP couldn't keep up with him. My insides buzzed in confusion.

"We should eat." Karl motioned to a servant, who brought out a spread that was more German smorgasbord than light brunch. Bloated pastries, hearty meats, cheeses, coffee, tea.

I poked at a black, thick sausage. "This looks . . . great."

Karl eyed the sausage. "Yes. Delicacy, there."

"Really? What kind?"

"Oh, you know what this is."

"Of course I do." I tried not to make a face. "I eat this . . . all the time."

"So . . . we should . . . dig in."

We stared at the flecks of fat inside. Karl's fungus seemed more appetizing.

A servant added another platter of cheese to the table. "Does His Highness approve of the *blutwurst*? It was made with alpine pig's blood." He slid a slice onto our plates. "Very delicious!"

The sausage reeked. Here I was trying to look beautiful and irresistible, when I'd much rather throw up. But this food wouldn't be foreign to Elsa. I knew I had to be Method. I stabbed a piece and held it up to my mouth, closed my eyes, and took a bite. It was worse than it looked—metallic and salty. Seriously, it took every ounce of strength I had not to spit it out. I swallowed.

When I opened my eyes, Karl was staring in amazement. But then he cut himself a thick bite and looked up at me with tragic regret, like he was about to eat poison. "If she can stand it, I can. Play it!" he said.

Wait, what? That's a line from *Casablanca*. Did he know that? I watched him chew the disgusting sausage and couldn't stop a strange feeling rising up in my throat. Not the sausage (gross!), but uncontrollable laughter.

He swallowed the bite and, in a perfect Humphrey Bogart impersonation, added, "Here's looking at you, kid."

I was laughing so hard now, I felt faint. Giddy. "I love that movie! I used to pretend my Ken doll was Humphrey Bogart."

He cracked a smile. "Sorry, doll. I don't think Ken could do Bogie justice. Nobody can. Hollywood stars now just don't have that same . . . you know."

"I *know*!" I leaned in. "And Ingrid Bergman! Did you

know Ann Sheridan was also considered for the part?"

"Oh, no. Ingrid Bergman was born to—" Karl froze. "I mean, I only watch movies like that when nothing else is on, of course. Because I'm too busy . . . hunting."

Good thing he stopped! *I used to pretend my Ken doll was Humphrey Bogart?* Describing my OWN memory—man, that was so amateur. Seriously, Desi.

Still, how cool that he knew *Casablanca?* The only movies guys in Idaho knew involved either lots of explosions or burping. Or both. And Elsa was right: when he spoke about AFRICA IS HUNGRY, he was just so *passionate*.

"Oh yeah, I'm not some movie buff or anything. I just watch when they have subtitles," I said. "I'm usually helping Nana Helga in the garden anyway."

Karl analyzed me for a bit, like he was planning something out, then stood up and walked purposefully over to me. He held out his hand. "Hey, you want to go for a walk or something? Speaking of gardens, let me show you ours. Totally incredible."

Chapter
19

I was seriously getting paid for this? I hadn't laughed so hard since Drake accidentally let a guinea pig loose in the mall. The gardens were, of course, phenomenal. Karl kept comparing all these plants to different royals and making me laugh. (See this shrub? Totally the Earl of Boden.) Actually, that's all I really did for the next two hours. Crack up. Who'd have thought Karl could be so . . . fun? Of course, I knew he was nice, but on TV and in magazines he'd always seemed a little stiff for me, not to mention our interaction the day before. I guess now that he was home and comfortable he was finally being himself. If this was the Karl that Elsa knew, I could maybe see where her crush was coming from.

Not enough to fill up a stalker notebook, but enough to start, like, a page.

Maybe a page and a half.

We wandered out of the formal gardens into an open field, our bare feet cushioned by the soft grass. The sun was out, the air smelled fresh, and I wouldn't have traded all the jewels in the world for an impact moment like this.

"So, video games, old movies, and a passion for goats." I bumped into him. "What would the tabloids say about that?"

"First off, I love the people I'm giving the goats to, not the goats themselves. No offense to goats. And the tabloids won't say a thing if you don't rat me out."

"'Rat me out'? You're starting to sound like a normal person. Are you trying to get on Nana Helga's good side?"

"Does she have one?"

"Very funny." I cleared my throat. "I do want to thank you for having me over for brunch."

"Who else would I have to hang out with here? Actually, I saw some goats in the village. . . ."

"No, I'm serious. Ever since my mom died, especially, and I've been all alone with Nana Helga, I've missed . . . this. Seeing you again means a lot to me. You mean a lot to me. It's like the good old days."

Karl fingered the leaf of a plant, avoiding my eyes.

"Elsa, I. . . . Maybe I should tell you this later." He rubbed the back of his neck and sighed.

"No, tell me now!" I almost yelled. "Or . . . or I'll hit you."

Karl closed my window of opportunity with a quick smile. "Hit me and I'll show you my fungus again."

"If you take off your socks, I'll strangle you with them." I paused. So much for a heart-to-heart. "You don't really have a fungus, do you?"

He grinned wider. "It's highly contagious. I touch you? You're gone. Fungus infected for life."

"Then I better not let you touch me." I bolted, laughing. On the hill was a solitary tree with a swing. I'd seen it before! Not the actual tree, but a drawing. In Elsa's notebook. I ran to the top and sat on the weathered board. "Push me?"

"Even with the fungus?"

"I'll risk it."

I eased on to the swing, and Karl gave me a gentle shove. Each time I floated back, Karl's hands brushed lightly on my shoulders.

"It's so pretty out today," I said.

Karl stopped the swing, his gaze focused on the midafternoon sun. "It is, but we should probably go back in soon."

"Oh." I stood up. "Sure. Sorry."

"Don't apologize. It's just . . ." He brushed his thumb along my jaw before he tugged on my hair. "You have a leaf in there."

I fingered the strand. "How embarrassing."

"Don't be embarrassed. I like your hair. I like it when you do it in braids too. I like—Oh, great. Here comes my brother."

I turned to see Prince Barrett striding up the hill. Every

nerve in my body went from a little tingle to hyperalert. Oh man, I'd almost forgotten about Barrett. But he was even better looking in person. Karl, who on his own was decent, looked straight-up wimpy next to Barrett, the Prince of Hot.

"What are you two crazy kids up to?" he asked.

I couldn't answer. I was staring. I couldn't stop. He was, like, seventeen. And a *celebrity*. One of *People* magazine's fifty most beautiful people two years in a row. You'd have to be completely Method to not be impressed by that.

"Elsa, you remember my brother, Barrett?"

Barrett nodded at me. "Of course she does. Now, Elsa, how is your *nana* doing?" he asked, emphasizing the word in an almost sarcastic way.

I tried to swallow, but my throat was too dry. Had his hotness dehydrated me? What was he saying about Nana Helga?

"She's . . . she's the same."

"Must be hard for you. Has she stopped pretending to be common yet?"

I blinked, and the spell broke for a moment. I definitely wasn't going to join the Nana Helga fan club anytime soon, but I didn't see why Barrett had to make fun of Elsa's family to her face, regardless of how right he was.

"She's—"

"Fine," Karl cut in. "And still Elsa's family, so you might want to apologize."

"Apologize? Why? What did I say?" Barrett shook his head, his shiny hair flowing in the breeze. *Sigh*. "I almost forgot. You left your cell phone in the entertainment room." He tossed Karl the phone. "Olivia called."

"Oh? What did you tell her?"

"That you were busy. You might want to call her back, though. She didn't seem too keen."

"She'll be fine," Karl said quickly.

Barrett's expression was all innocence. "Have you told Elsa here about the big announcement? My little brother, wooing the ladies while I have to sit back and live the quasi-single life. It's so very lonely."

I didn't say anything, just gripped the swing's ropes.

Karl snorted. "You're not even single."

"That's why I said quasi." Barrett winked at me.

"Give it up. Elsa's too young for you."

"Salt in the wound, brude." Barrett flashed a smile. "Salt in the wound."

Barrett left, and I enjoyed the departing view, his sexy cologne still hanging in the air. There was little celebration, however, in the come-on because it wasn't *my* looks he was noticing anyway. Plus, you know how some guys get less attractive once they open their mouth? It would take lots and lots of talking to totally diminish his cuteness, but maybe that's how Barrett was. While Karl, well . . .

Karl was kind of growing on me.

"So," I said.

"So," Karl sighed and plopped down on the grass next to the swing.

"So we might as well talk about Olivia," I said.

"Yeah? What about her?"

"You tell me. I'm not the one who's dating her."

An uncomfortable silence followed.

"Look, Elsa, there's really something you should know about that—" Karl's phone rang. Olivia's name flashed on the screen. "She'll just keep calling if I don't answer. Can you wait just a minute? I'll be right back."

He walked down the hill, back to the gardens, leaving footprints in the overgrown clover. I watched him and felt a pang of guilt.

This wasn't some Hollywood movie where things ended up happily ever after and the credits rolled. I was making choices—big choices—that would impact Elsa, Karl, Olivia, and who knew how many others. This was their reality. What if I was messing this all up?

Suddenly I wondered what Meredith would say. Already I could imagine our reunion. Not quite baskets of sunshine after all this. Unless . . . Really, I just needed time to think.

I stole one last look at Karl, then did the only thing I could. A little maneuver I like to call the Amazon Dash: I took off running into the house. The driver didn't say a thing when he saw me, just walked out and started the limo.

I wasn't even tempted to turn on the flat screen when I got inside the car. The movie of my life was providing enough drama to make an epic.

Chapter
20

Nana Helga was outside pulling weeds when we drove up to the house. The driver, Dieter, I'd learned, started to open his door to let me out, but I cleared my throat. "Hey, Dieter? I got it. Thanks."

Nana Helga eyed me stoically from underneath an orange sun hat.

Okay, so maybe Dieter should've dropped me off down the hill.

"You have a good time at brunch?" she asked, bending her head back down. Her lips puckered as she worked, perspiration creating a makeup line on her forehead. The humidity and distant gray clouds promised rain soon.

I kneeled down beside her. "It was okay. We just

walked around the gardens and caught up."

Nana Helga wiped her hands on her pants. "Come inside. There's something I want you to see."

She marched right in, not even bothering to stomp the dirt off her work shoes. Groceries poured off the counter. She rifled through a bag and slapped a magazine down in front of me. Duchess Olivia was on the cover.

"Thought you'd find this interesting."

I didn't pick it up. "I already know about that."

She tore through the pages until she found a picture of Karl and Olivia stepping out of a limo. She jabbed her finger at it. "Then why are you still chasing after him? His type thinks they're better than us. He'll just break your heart."

I pushed the magazine aside. "Have you ever thought I might break *his* heart? You can deny it all you want, but I *am* his type, Nana. I mean, I'm royal too, and we grew up together. Karl doesn't sell me short, so why do you?"

"You will not talk to me like that."

"Why not? I'm not asking for the world. Seriously, you won't even let me go to that polo match! Or hang out with the guy I've liked forever? Why?"

"You are just like your mother—"

"Well, good! Better that than pretending I'm penniless and angry all the time and scared to accept who I am—"

Nana Helga grabbed the magazine and shoved it into my chest. She walked outside, kicked a shovel, and cursed. I followed her, but she held up her hand.

"You've said plenty, *schatz*. I'm going on a mad walk now. Nothing like the smell of forget-me-nots to clear my head. You should do some cooling too."

I watched her walk away. Well, that was just fantastic. Not only had I failed at convincing Karl that Elsa was the girl for him, I also hadn't made any progress with Nana Helga. This dual campaign was blowing up in my face.

I sat down and thumbed through the magazine, stopping on Olivia's interview.

DUCHESS OLIVIA LETS GO by Brett Morgan

When Duchess Olivia walks into a room, everyone notices. And it's not the royal title that's getting the attention. Her long black hair bounces with each step. She's dressed for success in a brown herringbone pencil skirt and sheer blouse. As she sits down at our corner table at a trendy outdoor bistro and peels off her glasses, her emerald eyes look wise beyond her sixteen years. "Let's talk about me," she says. And so we do.

Duchess Olivia, first let me say what an honor it is that you would grant this interview. You're a major buzz girl, and here we are.

Yes. Here we are.

You're usually not too open with the press.

Well, can you blame me? I've been burned before, like that coverage when I wore fur. Horrible. It was one coat. Two, if you count that benefit in London, but it was Grammy's coat. I wore it out of love for her.

The rumors are swirling about your supposed relationship

with Prince Karl of Fenmar. Care to set things straight?

Ah, you must mean those yacht pictures. The girl in the bathing suit was Photoshopped and so not me. She was, like, over twenty and had cellulite!

But as far as Karl and I being together, yes! We are dating. We're still in that giddy new-relationship phase. He's so shy and tongue-tied around me, it's adorable.

His Highness works tirelessly for many nonprofit organizations. Have you joined in his efforts, or are you exploring other charities?

I haven't found the time yet to start my own. Now that I've taken some time away from academy, I'm focusing on my riding, and I'm splitting my time between New York, Paris, and Dubai, and . . . it's exhausting, really.

But I think Karl is precious when he goes on about AFRICA IS HUNGRY. *My mom and I are planning an A-list gala to raise awareness for the cause. It's going to be phenomenal.*

A-list. So Elsa would not be getting an invite to that, and like it would matter since she couldn't even go to a polo match. The interview went on, but I'd read enough. I stared at Karl in the picture. He wasn't looking at the camera—more past it. What are you thinking, Karl? She's more into herself than she is you.

It was tragic, really, that a nice guy like Karl would date Olivia. It was just like Hayden and Celeste. Well, maybe not *just* like. Karl was royalty, after all, and therefore naturally had better manners. And Hayden was, um, *Hayden.*

Which actually got me thinking: when I got back to Sproutville, whenever that might be, I'd still be in that dunk tank. If I stayed under the water, would Hayden do what Karl surely would—jump in and save me? I couldn't have wasted all those years adoring someone who would try to dunk a girl and leave her to drown.

Right? Because if so, maybe I was the one selling myself short.

I snuggled into a pillow and stared up at the ceiling, brainstorming all the ways to get Karl to change his mind. I was on solution seventeen: create a new reality show— *Royalty Island*. They'd have an elimination battle, and Elsa's mountain-girl biceps would dominate. Ooh! And Olivia without makeup probably wasn't pretty, and I bet the wild animals would instinctively go after her first.

I fell asleep with my finger still between the magazine pages.

Tap! Tap! Tap!

A rapid, urgent knocking woke me up. Elsa's dress rustled as I rolled off the couch and opened the front door. Karl stood shivering under the leaking front awning, his face barely visible in the dim porch light. The clouds, so distant earlier today, had roared in, assailing the house with rain.

"What time is it?" I asked.

"Late." His teeth chattered. "Can I come in?"

"Oh . . . sure. I'll make a fire. Take my blanket."

Karl waited on the welcome mat while I got the fire

going. When it was good and roaring, he sat down on the red brick, his gaze fixed on the flames. "So, why did you leave this afternoon?"

"You had to call your girlfriend." I sat down on the coffee table across from him and smoothed my hair. "I didn't want to overstay my welcome."

"You couldn't do that—I wish you had let me know you were leaving. I was worried you were mad."

"I wasn't mad. I'm just a little confused."

"You're wearing your locket," Karl said in wonder.

I straightened the chain. "I've had it on all day."

"You have? Yes, yes of course you have." He had a far-away look in his eyes. "I remember when I gave that to you. Do you recall what I said?"

"Remind me."

"I said to keep it empty because that's how I felt when you weren't around. Silly sentiment, wasn't it?"

"I don't think so," I said softly.

Karl reached out to touch the locket, but just as his fingers brushed the engravings, he drew back. I seriously wanted to rip it off and throw it at him for being so stupid. Elsa is right here! Don't make this a *Roman Holiday* ending where they love each other and walk away from it. You two can have the fairy tale. Just take it.

Rain battered the windowpane, the water cutting into the black night.

"Karl, what have you been trying to tell me? That we're over? If that's it, just say it."

"Over? Elsa, I could never be *over* with you. Trust me, I've tried and—"

Lightning flashed in the room, immediately followed by fierce thunder that shook the floor, shook the walls. I jumped.

Karl leaned over and grabbed my hand. "Are you all right?"

"Yeah. Wow. This weather." Our entwined fingers consumed my attention. "It's crazy."

The roof hummed with the torrent of rain. We didn't speak. If it thundered again, would Karl grab my other hand too?

"Anyway . . . look." Karl dropped my hand and began pacing. "I didn't mean to hurt you. But Olivia is—"

"Olivia is a legit royal. And I'm not, right? Oh, and she wears fur." I picked up the magazine and waved it. "There is no way this girl is for real. Seriously, Karl?"

He buried his face in his hands. "I've been so mixed up since I ran into you. I forgot about how it is to be around you. I'd convinced myself we were just kids before. . . . You have no idea how difficult this is. Like talking to, I don't know, your Nana. I mean, what I'm trying to—"

"Nana Helga." I sat up. "Karl, where is she?"

He paused. "I don't know. I haven't seen her."

"Oh no. She went on a mad walk before I fell asleep. She's out in this rain. Her heart. What if she slipped or—"

"I'll find her."

I snatched a pair of boots and a rain jacket from the closet. "No. She's my nana. We'll find her together."

Chapter
21

I shielded my eyes. I had to find Nana Helga. The rain no longer fell in drops, but in a massive sheet of water, an endless, pounding wave.

Karl ran out to the backyard, calling Nana Helga's name. I struggled to keep up in my too-large boots. The only answer we had was the howling wind.

"No!" I screamed. "Something has to be wrong. She's been out for hours."

"Everything will be fine." Karl set his jaw in determination. "You stay here in case she returns. I'm going to find her."

"No! Don't you understand? *I* have to save her. This is my fault! She left because of me. I'm supposed to be making a difference. A good difference."

Karl stared at me like I was crazy, then shook his head. "You aren't very easy to say no to."

"Then don't try it again."

We held each other up as we slumped through the mud, yelling her name until we both grew hoarse. Karl started to head down the hill toward the dim lights of the village when I remembered what Nana Helga had said before she left. "Forget-me-nots. Karl, Nana said they helped her calm down. There are flowers in the meadow."

We tripped up the path until we reached the meadow. Karl stopped me at the fence. "Wait here. That way, if I'm not back in a few minutes, you can go to the village for help."

I sank down into the mud and hugged my knees to my chest. Meredith was right. Blown-up bubbles weren't drama. This was. Totally created by me because I'd pushed so hard. If I hadn't yelled at Nana, if I hadn't taken a nap, if I hadn't gotten so wrapped up in the Karl saga, Nana Helga wouldn't be out there, in danger.

A few torturous minutes later, Karl stumbled up to the fence, Nana Helga's arm wrapped around his shoulder, a large gash on her forehead. She hit him relentlessly with her free arm.

I didn't realize I was holding my breath until I saw them. She was conscious, at least.

"I'm fine!" she said. "Seriously, I'm not some damsel in distress, here. Let me go."

Karl took the beating. We guided her through the grass and up the porch steps.

"What happened?" I asked, once Nana was safely inside.

She wiped some blood from her brow. "I got a little lost in the rain. And then fell down and got a small scrape. No big deal. This boy of yours flew in like he was Prince Charming—"

"You were lying facedown, almost unconscious in the meadow," he said.

"Just napping."

"Did you take your medication, Nana?" I asked.

She averted her eyes. "You going to scold me too? For the love, two children trying to take care of me."

"Let's dry you off."

Karl pulled out his cell. "I'll be right back. Dieter needs to pick me up anyway—I'll have him bring a doctor."

"I said I didn't need—"

He held up his hands. "Just in case."

Karl left to make the call, and I helped Nana Helga twist out of her wet clothes and into a dry nightgown. Once she was settled in bed, I found her medication and cleaned up her cut as best as I could. Karl wasn't back, so I sat at the edge of the bed and rubbed her cold feet.

"This pillow feels like it's stuffed with gooseberries," Nana Helga mumbled. "Mind giving it a fluff?"

I grabbed for her pillow, but she grabbed for me, swallowing me up in a hug. "I'm glad I went on that walk, *mein Schatz*. I was . . . Maybe I wasn't completely on target about the prince and other . . . issues. Like you wanting to be your own person . . . even if that means being royal. Maybe you could go to that polo match after all. You get what I'm saying?"

I swallowed back a smile at the closest thing to an apology I'd ever get. Impact number two: check. "Yeah. Sure."

Karl tapped softly on the door and poked his head in. "Dieter and the doctor are on their way, but it might take a while because of the roads. You think you'll survive?"

Nana Helga snorted and rolled away. "Surviving is what I do."

I found Karl some old work clothes of Nana's and excused myself to go clean up. I was just about to stick the brunch invite into Elsa's notebook when my rouge timer went off. Oh no. Time was almost up, and I still hadn't straightened things out with Karl. Eek! And what would Elsa do when she came home to find her long-lost love sitting in her living room? It was bound to be a disaster.

I grabbed my manual and rouge and was almost out the door when I had a thought. Flipping to the back of Elsa's notebook, I jotted down a quick sub report.

Elsa,

Hey, it's your sub, Desi. Hope you don't mind, but I found this notebook about Karl and figured you had a thing for him. Okay, "thing" is putting it mildly. Well, he happened to come into town while you were gone (!!!!, right?), so I worked on him a bit for you. No easy task considering he has the Duchess of Dental Floss. Get it? Because she wears those bikinis?

Anyway, I did help change Nana Helga's mind. She said you could go to that polo match you mentioned in your journal. (Uh, yeah. I read that too. All for a good cause!) You should keep on that with her. I think she might reconsider letting you be a part of the whole royal scene with enough work. And you totally should, Elsa. You're, like, <u>made</u> to be a princess.

Back to Karl. I'm not quite sure if I've broken through with him yet. Sometimes he seems to let his guard down, and he obviously cares a lot about you because he keeps coming by, and he seems really conflicted—like he can't let you go. Trust me, I know how it feels to like a guy and not be able to act on it. I really want to help. Action might just be the way to go.

More later!
Desi

Karl was sitting on the couch when I made it downstairs. I grabbed his hand and led him onto the covered porch. Dieter drove up in the limo. Time was almost up. I had to convince Karl that he wanted Elsa *and* get him out of there before she returned.

Still, despite the rush, the mood was very black-and-white movie. Two people unable to say what they really felt, time running out, and the rain . . . the rain was classic.

I could feel Karl watching me.

"Thanks for helping me save Nana Helga tonight," I said.

"Of course."

"I was kind of hoping we could finish our conversation."

Karl lowered his gaze. "Yes?"

"Yeah, I just . . . I really need to know what you're thinking."

He looked up at me again, and the look was enough to make any girl blush. Even if he was kind of short and not quite cute, his eyes could sure smolder. "Elsa, I . . . I care about you a great deal. A *very* great deal. But I have other people to think about. I have an image and a country and my parents and . . . I can't let my personal feelings cloud my duty and judgment."

Part of me, most of me, wanted to cry. Everything had been so great today at his house; why was he acting so formal and stuffy again?

We stared at each other for a moment, and suddenly something clicked in me. Looking at him, it was like my own heart started whirring, started filling with this need to show him he was wrong. Until I realized the whirring wasn't me, it was something farther off in the distance. Something like a traveling bubble about to appear. I rushed on as the rainy good-bye scene from *Breakfast at Tiffany's* flashed in my head. "You know what's wrong with you? You're chicken. You're staying with a girl because . . . because you're scared to break away from the expected. Is this what you, Karl—not your family or your country or the tabloids—really want?"

"No. It's what I . . . She's what I'm *supposed* to want. So please, let's make this as easy as possible. I know I initiated our contact, and I will cherish our time together, but everything has to go back to how it was. How it should be."

The whirring turned into a roar, like a helicopter was above us. Karl's hair swirled around his brown eyes, and his look was so confused, like he was smiling but sad and scared all at the same time.

There was only one way to convince him to let go of Olivia and find true happiness with Elsa. I just needed the guts to do it. "Things are not going to go back to how they were. Not once I do this."

And right in the middle of a wind tunnel, with a bubble crashing down next to us, I leaned in and gave him a kiss.

It—kissing—was a lot better than I'd ever imagined. Even if I wasn't in my own body, even though Karl thought I was someone else, and even though Meredith was about to wring my neck, it felt nice. Like it was only us. Karl, the rain, and me.

And Karl kissed me back! Well, for maybe five seconds he kissed me back, before pulling away and slapping his forehead.

"Elsa! That was wonder . . . but what are you . . . I thought today I . . . I have to think. Please excuse me." Karl turned and ran to his car.

I rubbed my still-buzzing lips. How could I have thought a kiss from me would convince him to leave a girl like Olivia? How could I have been so far off?

The bubble door opened and Meredith marched out onto the porch. Her green hair wisped loose from a ponytail. The only makeup she had on was mascara that was clearly left over from the night before. Most frightening, her green T-shirt—oh my gosh, she was wearing a T-SHIRT—was halfway tucked into faded black yoga pants.

"Desi, what are you doing?" She grabbed my shirt and almost lifted me off the ground. "It isn't your place to change things. THIS CAN HAVE GLOBAL REPERCUSSIONS!"

"I know, but I had to do *something*. Karl doesn't really like Olivia. He loves Elsa. I know it. And Elsa loves Karl. I might have changed things for the better. I'm sorry, but I was only trying to help."

"WHO CARES?" Meredith pushed me into the bubble. "Changing it for the better isn't any different from changing it for the worse. It's instability!"

"So . . . now what?"

"Now what?" A vein throbbed in Meredith's neck. "So now this prince thinks Elsa is in love with him, that's what. You don't think that's going to change things for Elsa? Plus, I have to somehow explain to her why her life's a mess!"

"She has a Karl love *notebook*. This is what she wanted. I promise."

"But she never acted on it. Wanting something and getting it are two different things."

"Look, I tried to e-mail you and check on this. It didn't go through because the server was down, and I had to go with my gut." Wait, maybe all wasn't lost. Meredith said she might keep me if I had good remarks. My Princess Progress Reports *had* to have something helpful and positive in them. They could save me! "Did you get my progress reports yet?"

"No! Carol's wedding was so crowded with subs it only jammed up the system more. I've never seen anything like it. Absolute nightmare. Besides, kissing Karl was a huge mistake. Big enough for them to rush your trial without PPRs. You're probably done for." She buried her face in her hands. "And you're so self-centered; who do you think is going to get blamed? The same person who gets blamed for every mistake you make. The same person who made the same stupid mistake and will spend the rest of her life paying for it."

"Wait, who are you talking about?" I asked.

"Me!" Meredith stomped her foot. "Me! Me! Me!"

Her phone rang. She checked the caller ID then dangled phone from her fingers like it was a dead rat. "Oh no. No no no. Not this. Not yet."

The ringing continued.

"Are you going to answer it?"

Meredith glared at me. "Yes. Plug your ears."

"What?"

"PLUG YOUR EARS!"

I stuck my fingers into my ears, and Meredith flipped open her phone. It made no difference. The voice on the other end nearly burst my eardrums.

"MEREDITH!"

"Oh hello, darling. How is your—"

"Court of Royal Appeals. Five minutes. And she'd better be ready to plead her case."

Chapter 22

Meredith didn't say a word to me as we zoomed away in the bubble. Which was so typical—send a girl to the depths of the Amazon or the middle of the Alps or the Court of Royal Appeals and give her no clue what to expect. Like I should just know. Like this was all something I'd been prepared for.

The shake, rattle, and roll of the bubble signaled our entrance into headquarters. The motion was nothing compared to the anger bouncing around inside me. Finally, when the bubble door opened and Meredith stepped out into the parking garage without so much as a glance in my general direction, I exploded.

"I didn't do anything wrong!"

She turned around slowly. Deliberately. "Let's rewrite that sentence. Desi, you did EVERYTHING wrong. I gave you a second, no, a third chance, and you blew it. So let's just get this hearing over with so I can take you home."

"Are you going to let me explain?"

"That's what the court is for."

We rushed up the parking garage incline. The rain in Paris was almost as thick as it had been in Metzahg. Meredith's umbrella was only big enough for her, so of course I got soaked all over again.

"Well, help me get my . . . my defense ready," I said, panting as we cut across a busy street.

"Desi, the fact that you even think you need a defense is the problem. During a normal Level Two trial, they analyze PPRs and debate whether you should advance. This is different. Another agent is assigned to investigate whether you should even remain with the agency. They show video to prove their point. The council deliberates. The end."

I froze. "You've *videoed* me?"

"Oh, keep walking. Of course we did. Not every minute, but random snippets are recorded by our Level One surveillance team. Plus, your magic sends signals to us when there are moments of high emotions. We just caught the tail end of the Nana Helga disappearance and were about to intervene when you found her. Then there was the little smoochie interaction you just had."

"And if I don't advance?"

"They pay you for your services and send you on your

206

way. Once you've been sub sanitized, of course."

We reached the building, and cute and dry Meredith whisked us through security and the modeling agency lobby, where I got a few sneers. Sure, I was a talent, but I also looked like I'd just stepped out of a dunk tank. Again.

"Sub sanitized?" I asked once we'd entered the second lobby and stepped into another elevator I hadn't noticed before, this one with *one* button. Down. "So I get a bath?"

"They wash your memory. You'll be put back in the dunk tank, and you won't remember me, or that prince, or any of this. You'll think some rich uncle died and left you the money. You'll go back to old Desi."

"They . . . they can't do that!"

"It's in the contract. In the fine print. Where we say we can do whatever we want."

I gasped. No. That couldn't happen. That could *not* happen. I did not walk through an Amazon fire and put myself out there for Elsa and the others for nothing. I would not go back to a life of fearing Celeste and trailing after Hayden. Forgetting everything I'd experienced would lead me back to vapor.

I was not vapor.

I mattered.

I spread my feet apart and firmly planted them on the elevator floor. I stared Meredith down. "No, Meredith. No. I'm going down kicking and screaming."

Kicking and screaming. Yes! I'd stage a protest. I plopped down on the ground. She would have to drag me out of here.

Meredith nudged me with the toe of her shoe. "Oh, don't be ridiculous. Get up."

"Look, you have been nothing but rude to me." I knocked her foot away. "You boss me around, treat me like I'm an idiot, and never say anything positive. And I'm sick of it. Lilith would have never been like this. I am not going to let you or this court or any princess take away from me what I just went through. So . . . there."

Meredith stepped back against the elevator wall like she'd been pushed. "Desi—"

"Save it. I'm done talking to you."

Meredith plopped down next to me. She didn't say anything for a little bit; I think she was still kind of shocked I'd stood up to her. Finally, she sighed, and when she spoke, her voice was soft. "Okay. Then I'll talk. I don't usually say this, but I'm . . . sorry." Her face pinched when she said that word. "I pushed you because I see more promise in you than I've seen in a long time. I knew you could take it. I was *preparing* you. You're right. Lilith wouldn't have treated you like this. She would have flitted in every ten seconds to tell you what to do, and would've never let you figure things out for yourself."

I snorted. "Yeah, a lot of good *that* did, right?"

"Look, either you have it in you to sub or you don't. That's the bottom line. If you didn't, you wouldn't have seen the ad. Millions of girls out there are not you. They couldn't do this. That girl at the mall the other day wishes she had your princessing skills."

"Celeste? How do you know about Celeste?"

"I know pretty much everything about you."

"I, but . . ." My voice cracked. I looked away so she wouldn't see me cry. "I don't want to forget all this. But I can't deny what I did. I kissed him and still think it was the right thing to do. Why even go to court? I'm obviously not going to pass."

"Persuade them that this subbing philosophy of yours actually works. You know, I was a lot like you at your age. There were some who strongly opposed my desires to change things within this agency, and they won out when I . . . I made a mistake. A big one. Like, take what you just did and multiply it by a million."

"You kissed a million princes?"

She laughed softly. "No. Just one. More than once, though. I . . . I fell in love with him. He was a friend of a princess I'd matched for, so I got to see him a lot, got to know him, and, well. When he told me he felt the same way, I finally told him who I really was. You can imagine how that went down with the agency. I'm lucky to have a job."

"Meredith, I had no idea. Wait, so where is he now?"

"Where he's always been. I had to turn him away after that, of course. All for the best. But hey, you're different." She leveled her gaze. "You *were* acting for your client, right?"

"Sure. Of course."

"Then make that clear in your trial. If you can reach

inside yourself, there's quite a bit of grit you can pull out. And you'll need it. You're ready for this."

And then Meredith hugged me. Well, she put her arm around my shoulder and gave it an awkward squeeze. And if I could get someone like Meredith Pouffinski to show emotion, maybe I had a chance in this court after all.

The elevator pinged open, and cold rushed in, swirling around me and grabbing my bare arms with force. The torch-lit room was dark. Dark as a dungeon. Oh, so maybe this *was* a dungeon. The eerie silence only broke with the occasional plunk of dripping water. We turned one corner, and the doors to the Court of Royal Appeals loomed before us.

"Do we knock?" I whispered to Meredith. My voice echoed against the rock walls.

"They'll come." She wiped her hands on her yoga pants, her eyes darting around the room as if she was . . . as if Meredith was *nervous*.

The doors—imported from some European castle, I guessed—were heavy, dark wood, with ornate, fairy tale–like carvings of dragons and knights and princesses, vines draping around the borders. For every carving of a princess, there was another girl nearby, peeking out from behind a tree, leaning out of a window. Watching. And waiting to start her next gig.

"They don't tell you about this part during orientation," I said.

Meredith brushed her fingers over the wood, her hands

trembling. "There's a lot they don't cover in orientation. And half of what they tell you is just propaganda. Like the stuff about Woserit, the priestess who died for her queen. Everyone knows she just tricked the murderer into drinking his own potion. But no, the martyr story fits perfectly with their silly save-the-queen theocracy and totally downplays how important the sub is, how we couldn't even exist without MP."

"So there's a whole different agency history?"

"Oh yeah. We totally had higher sub fatalities, harsher consequences. This was all before we were even located in Paris, and well before this building went up right on top of our underground offices. They introduced the court a few centuries ago to bring some order to the agency. They used to punish Sub Spottings by burning the poor girls at the stake."

"Do they . . ." I gulped. "Do they still do that?"

"It hasn't been abolished or anything."

"But subs are important. You don't want to lose them, right?" I asked.

"Subs have MP. And the ability to manipulate magic is what makes this agency money. At the end of the day, that's what they care about. They're very . . . careful to make sure MP is only used on royals."

"So . . . why not see how else magic could—"

The doors cracked open. A deep voice called out, "Desi Bascomb. ENTER."

I reached for Meredith's wrist. "Come on."

"No. No, I've got some work to take care of. I wonder if I could . . . " Tiny beads of perspiration formed on her forehead. Wait, Meredith *sweats*? "You go in."

"You're not coming in?"

"It'll be fine. I'll make an appearance later. You'll get by."

"Get by? I don't want to get by! My butt is on the—"

"Desi Bascomb? Now."

I clasped my hands like I was praying. "Meredith. Please help. I don't want to forget."

She was already walking away. I sighed and stepped into the room, looking back in time to see Meredith turn the corner before the giant doors slammed shut.

Chapter
23

I stood in a cavernous room with curving stone walls. In the flickering light of two torches, I could see only a few feet ahead of me. My footsteps echoed on the cobblestones as I stepped forward.

"Um . . . hello?"

The firelight went out, leaving me in complete darkness. Then I was flooded in a circle of light, which burned my eyes like eggs on a skillet.

"Desi Constance Bascomb. You are here to face the Court of Royal Appeals. Sit."

An invisible force pushed me into a wooden chair that appeared out of the blackness. The spotlight on me dimmed to darkness. Seven more spotlights lit up seven people seated at a crescent-shaped stone desk. The room was larger than I'd imagined—so big I could barely make out the features of the seven judges. Three men, four women, all identically dressed in black suits. Really, the only difference was their hair. Every head sported a different color of the rainbow. The woman in the center, whose seat was raised slightly higher than the rest, had every color incorporated into her style. I recognized her from the portraits I'd seen before. Genevieve.

The blue-haired judge spoke first. "Lilith will review the charges against you. After which, you will be given a sufficient amount of time to defend your actions. The court will then deliberate what your future holds. Do you have any questions?"

"Yes, well—"

"The correct answer is no."

"Oh, I'm sorry, really. I don't want to overstep my bounds here." Oh no, I *am* as dense as a drunk duke. Stop talking, Desi! "I didn't mean—"

"Just say no, Miss Bascomb."

"No. No questions. Sorry, I'm a little nervous here. None. Sir."

The spotlights on the Rainbow Council went out, and one appeared on another woman entering through the double doors. Lilith, curves fully on display in a lavender business suit, covered the expanse of the room in ten calculated steps.

Cool. If Meredith wasn't going to stick around, at least I

had Lilith reviewing the case. Actually, she was probably better than Meredith. Lilith was all roses and sunshine. She knew I could do this. She'd trained me. Salvation!

I grinned at her.

She returned my smile with a cold, blank stare. Pulled out a stopwatch, clicked the buttons twice, then leaned in and whispered in my ear. "I like to guess how long it takes the surrogate rejects to crack. You should have followed my teaching better. I gave you three minutes, Desi dear. I was being kind."

My smile evaporated. *WHAT?* She was not a warm, caring, dream agent. She was Façade's version of Anne Baxter in the fifties movie *All About Eve*—a double-crosser! And my professional future rested in her hands.

Ta-ta, dream job.

"Your Honors," she said, her elitist accent caressing the words. "I've reviewed this case and, frankly, I'm surprised we even need to meet. There is no doubt Desi has left a wake of destruction in her short time with the agency, despite the excellent training she received. Now, the footage was extensive, so I edited it to display the major blunders. I'll warn you—it's graphic."

A massive movie screen lowered from the ceiling. Lilith yanked her purple controller from her clutch and pointed. An image of Simmy's palace filled the screen.

"Here we have Desi's first assignment, Princess Simmy, an . . . amply built, quiet princess with an odd duck fetish. Desi was instructed to drift through this like Simmy drifts through her life. Instead, this happened."

She clicked a button on the remote, and the scene where I demanded food played out.

"Clearly, not in character. Here she is at her next assignment, an Amazon tribal dance. I believe the footage will speak for itself."

My image came on the screen again, this time in eagle feathers and black paint, a look that did nothing for Ama's waist. They'd at least had the decency to cover up my/her chest with one of those black bars. The footage started after the fire dancing part. (Of course they skipped that. I nailed the fire dancing.) The eagle guys did their thing, and then I began to dance. And I still think I rocked it, but it didn't matter so much what I thought as what the villagers thought, and the confused expressions on their faces proved they were not quite ready for the funk.

Lilith shuddered when I broke out the Cabbage Patch, and stopped the tape. "Sorry I can't give you back the last thirty seconds of your life, Your Honors."

If I hadn't been rooted to my seat by some invisible force, I would have challenged Lilith to a dance-off right there. I'd like to see *her* perform the Cabbage Patch and Lawn Mower in precise syncopation with the drummers.

"An emergency bubble was sent for this job. Meredith claims the accident resulted from a malfunction, but that does not explain Desi's absence afterward. To be honest, this whole situation doesn't seem right to me—"

"Lilith. Meredith has already turned in the required

paperwork, and it's been cleared." Blue-haired judge's voice was firm. "Let's move on."

"Yes." Lilith smiled sweetly. "Let's."

So the bubble crash didn't show up on my file? Whoa, I did not understand that lady. She covered for me with the bubble thing, didn't mention my leave time, but then left me to fry?

"Finally, her last job, which clearly displays her blatant disregard for the agency's policy of not influencing the princesses' lives. Although initially the gravity of this offense may not be apparent, I believe the agency's oversight that resulted in Prince Karl's . . . status is not relevant here. Of course, that unique situation will be analyzed separately."

Unique situation? Status? I get it. He's a prince. I'm not. I mean, Elsa isn't. I mean, a princess. Technically.

The mention of Karl stung. Thanks to the unfolding court drama, I'd temporarily forgotten how we'd said good-bye.

"Who is to say Desi will not repeat her mistake shown here?"

Lilith played the footage in all its humiliating glory. I closed my eyes when I knew it was coming, but when I snuck a peek, the picture was still there, frozen on the moment before Karl pulled back. And I know it was supposed to be incriminating evidence and all, but the image actually proved what I'd previously not dared to believe.

Because at that precise immortalized moment, Karl's eyes were closed too.

Yes! I knew it. I *knew* I'd done the right thing. So what if I'd done it without Elsa's permission? It was her secret desire. They were right for each other. They could work it out. Adios, Olivia! Princess Impact had left her mark. Job or not, I'd still done something right.

I closed my eyes and remembered the kiss. I could feel it now, feel him kissing me back.

Well, kissing *Elsa* back.

Lilith's stopwatch went off. "I'm not going to waste the court's time with a lengthy discourse. The evidence is as clear as the crown jewels at afternoon tea. Desi is not Level Two material. I recommend a proper sub sanitation."

"Sub sanitation? I . . . I kissed a boy! For my client!"

"Your recommendation will be noted, Lilith, although ultimately it's the council's decision. Thank you." The orange-haired judge looked at me and, I think, smiled. "The time is now yours to plead your case, Desi. We'd like to hear in your words what happened, particularly with Prince Karl."

"I don't know what to say. I mean, I kissed him, yeah. And this might not matter, but"—I pointed to the screen— "he kissed me too. His eyes were closed. I haven't kissed many boys, well ANY other boys, but if he closed his eyes, I think it means he didn't hate it, right? So maybe he actually felt something for me . . . for Elsa. Anyway. Maybe I did something that would've happened on its own."

"Is that your only defense?" Blue Hair asked.

My defense. I took a deep breath. "I did my research on

this—I read Elsa's diary, really got to know who she is and what she wants. And she wanted Karl. That's why she even got a sub, because that *wanting* was too much for her to handle. The thing is, I took this job because I wanted to make an impact. At first it was more about me, like being glamorous and confident and like Grace Kelly. But somewhere along the way, I decided I needed to figure out how to take a stand for people who might want to do it themselves, but never had the nerve. If I had someone subbing for me at home, I'd love it if they told off my enemy and kissed my crush. Stepping in and giving a princess a vacation is one thing, but stepping in and giving her the courage to improve her life, isn't that better?

"I'm not saying I didn't make mistakes. I'm still learning, and I really hope I can learn more in Level Two. I probably wasn't Method enough, and I probably got too involved in these girls' lives sometimes, and maybe my whole time as a sub was just one big mistake, and none of the princesses liked me. But I honestly believe that if you consider my performance overall, you'd see that I was trying to do what these girls really needed. Change is, um . . . good."

"I should have let her plead her case first." Lilith snorted. "What a bunch of idealistic drivel."

"It's called *using your mind*, Lilith. You should try it."

Out of nowhere, Meredith, in black leather pants with a green flouncy blouse, was standing right next to me. Meredith, who had said she had other work to do, who was always too busy for me, had come to save the day. Unless she had come to watch me destroy myself. I could imagine her enjoying that.

"Meredith." Lilith clapped her hands. "So glad you could overcome your little phobia to join us."

"Well, thank you, Lilith. I'm actually late because Hank came up with a solution for the interface problem. He really needed a hand. You all know how technology can react with magic. Anyway, the new PPR system is finally working, so we can include the princesses' take on the matter too."

"Of course." Lilith eyed Meredith with a mix of respect and disgust. "The more evidence, the merrier."

Meredith disappeared from the spotlight for a moment and whispered to someone or something in the darkness. Lilith tapped her foot, and I stared in the direction of the judges, doing my best to read their minds. Or perform telepathic voodoo. Just close the case.

Close. The. Case.

"All right." Meredith's voice was all sugar, like she was on the phone with a client. She even slid her arm protectively over my shoulder. "Let's watch Desi's Progress Report from Princess Simmy, the princess Lilith claims Desi incorrectly impersonated."

The Webcam video rolled, and there was Princess Simmy seated at her desk, her duck mobile dangling over her head.

"How would you rate your sub's performance and why?" asked a computerized male voice behind the camera.

Simmy beamed. "I'd give her a five."

"A five out of ten?" the man asked.

Thanks, Meredith, and this footage was supposed to help me how?

Simmy laughed. "Oh, sorry. I got mixed up. I meant a five out of five. Or a ten out of ten. I would give her a perfect!"

"Why's that?"

"Because she gave Nabila a piece of her, uh, *my* mind. I've always wanted to do that, and now because Desi started it, I'm standing up to her too. And I'm feeling better about myself and taking care of my body. Plus, I love Queen Raelena and I'm scheduled for all kinds of performances on my French horn. Can I can send my sub something as a thank-you—maybe a box of dates?"

My stomach twisted. Dates. Some subs get tiaras. I get dates. But wow. That was pretty excellent hearing feedback like that. And Simmy looked so happy!

"Oh, come on," Lilith said. "So she made a lucky mistake. Still doesn't change the fact that she was going against our age-old rules of impersonation. The rules *I* dutifully taught her, by the way. When you take into account the hard evidence—"

"Good idea, Lilith. Roll the next tape, please."

The next video came on, featuring Princess Ama, still wearing her ceremonial attire, surrounded by rain forest. Holy blow darts. I was about to get it.

The interview was in Ama's language, with subtitles in English. "I love sub girl much! It was an affectionately personal touch she did go out of her road and meet me and somehow smooth this worry over with my dad. And Tereis love the dance! He said it had otherworldly and spirit essence toward it. Oh, and my whole village was so excite about the visit tree spirit. So winning for everyone!"

See? Awesome dancing. And note to self: the little things count. Who would have thought smiling to her dad could impact so much? I guess impacting doesn't always have to be something major.

"Okay, we get it." Lilith yawned. "So she has good progress reports from two nobody Level One princesses. We still don't have her PPR for Elsa, and you can't explain away Desi's romantic rendezvous. But you know how that goes, don't you, Meredith?"

Meredith shrunk into herself for a moment, then shook her head. "Now, Lilith. You don't see me bringing up your past mistakes, like those awful feathered bangs, or when you drove the Duke of York's car into a lake—"

"On topic, Meredith," Orange Hair scolded, although she sounded like she was smiling when she said it.

"Of course. Let's examine Desi's final position, shall we? While I don't have the PPR yet, there is this footage from the night Desi left."

The room filled with the audio before the picture came on. The howling and wailing of the storm vibrated on the stone walls. Seconds later, a graying image appeared on the screen. Through the mist and darkness, you could see me running in the rain, looking quite crazy, actually. Then it cut right to me sitting next to Nana Helga's bed, rubbing her feet.

"Desi helped save Nana Helga's life," Meredith said softly. "No one trained her for something like that. Desi truly performed as a princess should."

"And how do you account for her snog-fest after that?" Lilith sneered. "She was obviously seeking out her own wish fulfillment, and I'm not going to stand here and—"

"Careful, Lilith," boomed the richest, most regal-sounding voice I'd ever heard.

"Genevieve, I was trying to—"

A spotlight shone on the rainbow-haired woman standing in the middle of the court. Genevieve, with her long neck, even gaze, and commanding stance, looked very much like a queen ruling her kingdom. Except for, you know, the Bozo the Clown hairdo. "I know exactly what you were trying to do. Now, I think we have sufficient evidence from both sides of the case. The court will deliberate. Lilith, Meredith, and Desi, you may wait in the hall until we have reached our verdict."

Meredith kept her arm around my shoulder as we left the courtroom.

"That was a weak effort," Lilith said, once we were alone in the hallway.

"It was, Lilith." Meredith flashed her most dazzling of smiles. "I thought you'd have given a better case for the prosecution."

"Oh, Meredith. You look so radiant when you're wrong."

Meredith squeezed my shoulder. "This girl's a survivor. You're just jealous you're not representing her."

She pulled me far away from Lilith and gave me hug. "That was a struggle. I haven't been back to the court since I had my own appeal after that . . . *thing* with my prince. Since then, I've always had someone serve as my counsel for my subs. But I knew you needed me. I just had to get your PPRs first."

"You were amazing."

Meredith stood up a little taller. "I was, wasn't I? Wow, I can't tell you how good it felt to talk to Lilith like that."

I thought of Celeste and her little heart-shaped face. "I'll bet."

The doors opened. "We've reached our verdict." Genevieve's voice echoed. "You may enter."

Chapter 24

I swallowed. They couldn't have deliberated more than five minutes. Dad always said that when your case is weak, you want the jury out as long as possible. It means they're weighing out both sides. Even Celeste Juniper's dad got two hours before they sent him to jail.

I cast a sideways glance at Meredith, her chin up and eyes defiant. At least she came through for me in the end. I'd have to make sure and thank her before they wiped my memory of her. And Karl.

"We have reached a verdict. Desi Bascomb, approach the council."

Oh boy. I shuffled across the room, scared they might zap my brain right then and there.

Genevieve was frailer than she seemed from a distance. Still distinguished, but there was a kindness in her eyes. "You've had a very long day, haven't you, Desi?"

I nodded.

"I knew a Desi once. Of course, he was a Spanish prince, and the Desi was short for Desiderio. Latin for 'desire.' And did he ever live up to his name."

The red-haired man next to Genevieve coughed.

"My point is, I see desire in you too." Genevieve tilted her head. "You're obviously rough around the edges, but I don't think one mistake has to define us. You remind me of Meredith, actually, and she has grown to be a fine agent, one who perhaps I have overlooked in her talents. She sees promise in you, and based upon the evidence she presented, the court does as well. Your change theory certainly goes against our traditions, but it obviously didn't go against the princesses' wishes. And perhaps we give too much power to the royals and not enough to the surrogates. MP is a dying commodity, after all. That's all something for us to consider in the future.

"With that said, we have decided to allow you to continue with the agency with your memory intact, and progress to Level Two."

"Genevieve, let's reconsider this." Lilith cleared her throat. "She's a sweet girl, truly, but a bad apple can spoil the entire framework of this agency."

"No one is perfect, Lilith. Not you, nor I, nor even the royalty we represent. What we considered was her heart and drive. And I see great things in her future."

"Well, I can't argue her excellent training." Lilith narrowed her eyes at Meredith and me. "Ladies, best of luck in Level Two. I'm sure I'll see you again, Desi dear."

"Ta-ta, darling." Meredith wiggled her fingers at Lilith's back. The door slammed behind her.

"If there's nothing else"—Genevieve gave a slight nod—"then you two are dismissed as well."

"Actually." My voice cracked. "If it's okay, I wanted to know, um . . . So when does the Elsa PPR come in? I want to make sure everything worked out."

"We don't have Elsa's Princess Progress Report in yet, but the royal gossip chains indicate there's no lasting damage done. Prince Karl left Metzahg to join his girlfriend. I'm sure all will go back to how it was. Don't worry about that."

Back to how it was? Like I hadn't even been there, hadn't even mattered? Suddenly I didn't care about the trial. I may have made it through the court, kept my job and memory, but I'd failed Elsa. I'd taken a chance for nothing. What was the point of doing the right thing when the end result was so wrong?

"There is one thing you might want to know," Genevieve added. "Elsa was spotted in the village dress shop with her Nana Helga, buying something for an upcoming polo match. Just a little tidbit—thought you'd want to hear."

I smiled weakly. So she didn't have Karl, but she might get her debut. And maybe that debut could help her get Karl down the line. It was a seed—one that I'd planted. "Oh. Good. Thanks."

"Thank you for your kindness and understanding, Your Honors." Meredith curtsied. "I will guide my client out."

Meredith glided from the room with me slumping behind her. Her calm demeanor evaporated the moment the doors closed behind us.

"Desi! Oh, did you see the look on Lilith's face? Did you? And in front of Genevieve!" Meredith tapped her feet together. I think it was a happy dance. "And these tapes, the footage! I'm almost glad this happened, because I finally got to see—everyone did!—how fantastic you are. A royal role model!"

Her bouncing was making me dizzy. I steadied myself against the damp wall. "Role model?"

"Yes! And you've inspired me to do something I should have done a long time ago." She opened her phone. Still all business. "I can't believe I'm doing this." Her fingers pounded out a text. A very long text.

I traced the carving of the princess sub on the door. Funny, the prince and princess in the mural were smiling, but the sub was not.

Karl had left Metzahg. He'd kissed me, left town, and gone home to another girl. Eyes closed or not, that kiss had meant nothing to him. I'd thrown away my first real kiss on a guy who was with someone else.

Although, what did it matter? I'd been an actress in that movie, playing a part. He was and would always be with someone else. Whether that someone else was Olivia or Elsa, it still wasn't me. I could never have him.

Oh my gosh. Had I just *thought* that? I didn't want Karl! He was short and dorky and cowardly, except for at the house when he was funny and charming. I'd never had a good conversation with a guy like that, never connected. And his eyes were so . . . deep.

"There!" Meredith triumphantly waved her phone above her head. "It's done. Now he knows how I feel, how I still feel." She lowered her phone and grabbed my elbow. "You didn't see that happen, okay? I know I'm not the best example in that aspect, but you have no idea what it's like to love someone you can never be with. I can trust you, right?"

"Actually, I might have an idea what that's like."

I felt sick. Sick sick sick. How had I let this happen? How had I mixed business with pleasure? How much of my desire to impact Elsa had really been my own wish to get close to Karl? Well, I'm a professional. I'll just have to get over it. I won't think about that time we held hands by the fire, or his *Casablanca* reference, or the walk through the gardens, or . . .

The kiss.

Well, there goes that plan. There was no way on earth I could *ever* forget that kiss.

"You do know? Oof! I forgot. Your little hometown crush. Let's get you back to him, shall we? I always find that my subs' social lives improve after Level One. Confidence, I suppose."

I opened my mouth, hoping words could somehow explain my change of heart. It wasn't gorgeous-self-assured-clueless-paper-copying Hayden. It probably hadn't been since the Dunk of Doom. I mean, Hayden had thrown a ball when I was in the dunk tank.

He actually *liked* Celeste Juniper.

You know what, he probably CHEATED at Boggle. And he so wasn't Paul Newman.

I didn't want a Hayden anymore. I wanted a Karl.

"Maybe," I finally answered. I might be stupid enough to crush on a prince, but no way was I going to tell Meredith right now. Besides, a revelation like that might bar me from future Karl encounters. And as bittersweet and weird and hard as it would be to spend time with a great guy who liked me when it wasn't really *me*, I wanted to see Karl again. Even if I was just an actress in his and Elsa's great romance, it was still a part I wanted to play again and again.

"Well, we've got some time before I send you home for your Level One transition break." Meredith hit the elevator button. "You want to visit the Eiffel Tower or anything? I could give you a tour of Versailles. Major historical inaccuracies going on there."

"Maybe next time," I heard myself saying. "I want to go home. I miss my family. A break sounds like a really good idea, actually."

"Fine. A little time to recharge your batteries, then we'll start your Level Two training." Meredith pointed her phone at the open elevator, and the bubble appeared inside. She smiled sheepishly. "Going up? Small protocol break, but let's get you home."

This ride seemed shorter than the others. I was minutes away from being back where I'd left off, yet galaxies from being the girl I was.

I was Level Two now, after all. Level Two and thinking about an unavailable prince.

The bubble bounced, and we stared at each other. "There's your stop. Your paycheck will arrive very soon. When you're ready to get back to work, we'll be in touch."

"Sure. Yeah. In a few weeks. Or months."

"Lovely. Unless a gig comes up screaming Desi, in which case I'll contact you. Until then." She held out her hand.

"Don't you think we should hug or something?" I asked.

She hesitated. "This top. It's dry-clean only, and—"

I seized her in a hug. She gave my back a light tap. "You'll be right back in the dunk tank once you step through. Take a deep breath. There can be up to a one-minute delay, and given how long you've been under already, you could drown."

"Drown?" I pulled away.

Meredith laughed. "Enough with the drama."

I sucked in as much air as I could and flashed her a thumbs-up. I fell through the wall, back into a wet oblivion.

Chapter
25

*A*lmost drown? Is blacking out before hearing a name calling from the Great Beyond ALMOST drowning? Seriously, when I go back to that job, I'm so negotiating life-insurance benefits.

"Wake up, Desi!" a voice warbled. "Wake up!"

Someone's lips closed around mine and filled me up with air. I rolled to my side and coughed up water. A loud sound, almost like a cheer, filled my ears.

"Desi! Desi! Honey, can you hear me?"

I opened my eyes. My mom and Drake were peering down at me.

"Your dress. It's soaked." I coughed again. "Did I ruin it?"

Mom slowly pulled me up into a sitting position, her arm

around me. "A dress is replaceable. You aren't. What happened? Why didn't you swim or stand up?"

"I guess I was just traumatized," I said.

Mom tilted her head to the side, revealing a large crowd of onlookers. Come one, come all to the Idaho Daze fair—funnel cake and drowning girls, sure to be a smash! The HMs lingered in their tight circle, along with that new boy, Reed. Hayden, however, had peaced out.

Man, he dunks me and doesn't have the *decency* to stay and watch me cough up the water I almost drowned in. Not that I wanted anyone to witness my aqua-regurgitation, but still. What a waste of doodling space. He was so out of Karl's league.

Celeste stood just behind my mom, hugging herself. Celeste in her red dress with her pretty face and severe panty lines. Now would be the time to show my mom what Celeste was really like—to show everyone. Our eyes locked for one bazillionth of a second, but in that second, every memory I had of her, the good and bad and the years in between, played out, and I made the decision I never thought I would. I decided to let it go.

I let it all go.

"Yeah, well, I'm fine now."

Celeste's smug expression melted into a mystified O. The look I'd probably had on my face when I realized she was going to dunk me.

"I should take swimming lessons or something," I added. Celeste grabbed the HMs, her face still masked in confusion. Annie and Nikki nodded at me but followed Celeste. And I was okay. Maybe someday they'd break free. And if not, well, their loss.

"Here's a towel." Drake tossed me a *Finding Nemo* beach towel, and Mom wrapped it around me. "I'm really sorry. Next year we'll do a cakewalk. Actually, cake sounds good right now. I'm going to go walk until I win. And I'll save you a piece, okay, Desi?"

I laughed and nodded. When Drake was gone, Mom swallowed me in a hug. She smelled like summer and Vaseline. I nestled into her.

Then she wiped a tear from her cheek. "I want you to know I'm so proud of you."

"Proud of a pooper-scooper?"

"Proud of your hard work and guts. I would never have stepped into a dunk tank at your age. You're just so confident. I wish I was more like that."

"Um, thanks?" Had my pageant-queen mom seriously just complimented my confidence? What bizarre universe had I flown back to? "Where's Dad and Gracie?"

"They're at the petting zoo. I was just walking by and saw you lying on the ground, with that boy giving you CPR, and . . ." Mom's eyes welled up. "Oh, honey. I was so scared."

"Wait. Rewind." I glanced around to make sure Hayden wasn't around after all. Maybe I'd underestimated his chivalry. "Boy? CPR? Oh gross, it wasn't Drake, was it?"

Mom covered her mouth. "Oh! I almost forgot to thank him!"

She rushed over to Reed and pulled him back toward me. Hold up. He was the one who . . . Kylee was going to die. The new kid gave me MOUTH-TO-MOUTH?

"This boy helped pull you out of the water and gave you CPR." Mom turned on her smile. "You're a hero. Thank you so much for saving my daughter."

Reed ducked his head. "Was nothing."

Kylee was right. His accent was cute.

Mom patted my arm. "Well, I'm going to run over and find your dad and Gracie. Do you want anything? A funnel cake? Some dry clothes? Your makeup is smudged a little, honey—"

"I'm fine, Mom."

My mom left, along with the crowd, leaving just Reed and me alone. He squatted down next to me, the water from the dunk tank casting a swirly glow on his face. "So, rough day? You feeling all right? I'm Reed, by the way."

"Desi. Thanks. I'm fine." And, by the way, Reed, I think your lips were just on mine. Nice to meet you.

"I don't know many girls who would brave a dunk tank."

"Well, it was pretty harrowing."

Reed laughed an easy laugh that rose right from his belly. "Maybe you could go around to different schools and share your experience with other dunk tank survivors."

"Yeah, I'm sure there are millions of us." I squeezed some water out of my hair, amazed I felt as good as I did.

Mouth-to-mouth is like kissing, right? How could we just sit here chitchatting like this? I went from never kissing

235

a boy to multiple lip encounters in a day. Both technicalities, being as one was in another girl's body, and Reed had just been trying to save my life. But still. Go, Desi.

"Hey, do you want me to get you another towel or something?" Reed asked.

"I'm fine. My hair's probably a mess, though."

He brushed his hand across my chin and tugged at a braid. It was an odd gesture, considering we'd just met, but he'd earned it with the life-saver thing. "I like your hair."

"What did you say?"

"Your hair. I like it." His smile reminded me of Karl's. "Braids are cute."

I closed my eyes and shook my head. Stop thinking about Karl.

Kylee darted out from behind the milk toss and waved. "Desi! I just heard. Did you seriously pass out?" She stopped and gazed at Reed, her mouth open. A sound came out, but not quite a word.

"Sorry?"

"I'm Kylee."

"Reed."

"Wait, so did you—" Kylee pointed at Reed and then at me. "Desi, did he?"

I glanced at Reed. "Offer me a towel? Yep, he sure did."

"Seriously, though, let me grab you another one," Reed said.

Kylee waited until he was gone before she asked, "Okay, I heard there was CPR—"

"Yeah, but I was passed out, so it doesn't count—"

"No way. That totally counts. Oh my gosh! So did Hayden see you like that?"

"I don't care," I said. "I'm over him."

"Wait. You're over him? Uh, did you knock your head in the tank? You're sounding sane."

"I'm just listening to your advice. Finally."

"Good. You deserve better. Like, I don't know, the guy you just technically kissed. The one who saved your life. And if you're not taking him, I'm *so* next in line."

Right, because another boy was just what I needed. No way. Not after clueless Hayden and totally unavailable Karl. If I didn't have two jobs already, I'd be interviewing at convents.

"Step right up," I whispered, wishing with every last ounce of MP in me that I could tell Kylee about Karl so she'd understand.

Reed came back with a towel and handed it to me.

Kylee smiled flirtatiously and asked, "So, Reed. I'm dying to know what you think of Sproutville."

Reed grinned. "Feels like home already."

I came up with some project ideas and spent the next day designing a new T-shirt. Mom even gave me one of her nicer Gap ones—cream with puff sleeves. I freehanded a butterfly, then did the print in a clear, cursive font. I was going to do PUPA YOURSELF, but it sounded like POOP ON YOURSELF, and I'd had enough poop experiences via Pets Charming to last for eternity. What I ended up with was LIFE IS FREER ONCE YOU'RE OUT OF THE COCOON.

Instantly my new favorite shirt.

There was something else subbing had inspired me to do—and no, it wasn't a Karl notebook. I'm not into self-torture, although I did cut out one picture of him from a royalty magazine and stick it next to Paul Newman on my Wall o' Awesome Things. Just as a, you know, souvenir.

What I really wanted was to keep a journal, but write it kind of like it was fictional, so if anyone ever found it, they'd think it was just a bunch of fluff. Something to daydream in while I returned to normal life (including Pets Charming. Okay, so maybe I do like torture. But I had to help Drake protect his magical fish, right?). I'd detail how I'd impacted my clients, and brainstorm possibilities to help more, once I went back to the agency. Maybe write a little this or that about Karl. Research.

I rifled through my desk in pursuit of a clean spiral notebook. In the top of my bottom drawer I found a green envelope with sparkling ink. A purple, glittery credit card slid out. I held it up to the light, smiling as I read the enclosed note.

Desi,
Here is your pay for three gigs. If you want to know how it's broken down, e-mail me at mPouffinski@Facadeagency.com and I'll send you the details. Or, you could save me the time of doing the exchange rate, and know it's all in there, minus

taxes, my cut, and a percentage from the first two gigs to cover the Blow Dart Incident. As was stated in your contract, you are underage and unable to receive complete payment in cash. We don't want worried parents knocking down our door thinking we're running an underground drug ring. So, a Façade scholarship has been set up in your name, and you will receive four thousand dollars toward the college of your choice when you turn eighteen. Yes, we take education very seriously at Façade, and if you ever want to go corporate, you will need at least a bachelor's degree. The remaining six hundred fifty-eight dollars has been set up in a bank account accessible only by using the enclosed credit card. It's up to you if you want to show your parents this, but it might be hard to explain how a teenager qualified on her own. Might be best to keep this between us. It has been a pleasure working with you, and I look forward to furthering your employment with Façade. Until Level Two . . .

Ta-ta,
Meredith

Acknowledgments

If my life were made into a movie—*The Lindsey Leavitt Story Revealed*—I'd cast the following people as Those Who Made This Book Possible. (A collective role, but it's as meaty as they come. Even Audrey would be jealous.) Thanks to . . .

Sarah Davies a.k.a. The Literary Jerry McGuire. Desi would never have found her lovely home without your editorial guidance and keen business savvy. Ever since you took those boots off your desk, you've been running around on my behalf.

Emily Schultz, this book would be completely and quite literally void of magic if it weren't for your enlightened ideas and tireless efforts to get every last word right. I'm so very grateful for the opportunity to work with you, mighty OMEGA. The wonderful team at Disney-Hyperion Books for working so hard to make this book a success, especially Elizabeth H. Clark for a glamorous cover and Hallie Patterson for help with publicity.

Rachel Boden for your lovely input and for sharing the greatest princess story of them all. Alison Dougal for your grace and assistance. Also, thanks to everyone else at Egmont UK for all your work on the other side of the pond.

My mom for your constant cheerleading, support, and friendship. I'm sure there isn't a literate soul safe from your maternal salesmanship. And dad for *Sabrina*, *Rear Window*, *Funny Face* . . . and help with all the references in this text. And to you both for installing in me a love of books and believing in me and . . . Glitter!!!

Curry, who started this all by saying, "If anyone could be a writer, it's you," and riding the writing roller coaster with me, hands up. Also, for all the meals cooked, dishes cleaned, bedtime stories told while I went into my writing comas. Nothing hotter than a man in an apron, babe.

My girls for endless princess inspiration, playing so well together, and for not sighing too loudly when Mommy abandoned the puzzle just to "write one tiny thing down."

Uncle Kyle for buying me my first chapter book, *Ramona Quimby, Age 8*, and many more beyond that. Also, I'm sure you'll start the first and only middle-aged male fan club for this book, so I thank you in advance for that.

Brett, Zach, Morgan, and Rachel for the sibling support. And to the rest of my family: The Taylors, The Orrs, The Harrises, The Leavitts: Many of you will find your name in some form in the text of this very book. To the rest of you—don't worry. Many books to come. Just be nice, or I'll make you a villain.

Lisa Schroeder, you pushed me to finish this book, pushed me to submit it, and now here this is thanks to you, book angel. Lisa Madigan for getting me through the Great Halloween Agent Rejection of '07, as well as for the weekly e-mails and laughter. The Tenners, Holly Westland, Becca Fitzpatrick, Kay Cassidy, Rachel Hawkins, Irene Latham, Alexa Martin, Ginnie Johnson, Tyra Williamson, Sarah Johnson, Cynthia Jaynes, Angela Cerrito, Maurene Hinds, Shelley Seely, and Sascha Zuger. Thank you for your critiques and thoughts on everything from Amazon rituals to peanut allergies, and especially, *especially* for your friendship.

The wonderful people at Highlights Foundation for giving me a scholarship and a week in Chautauqua that changed my writing life. And, of course, the readers. Your contribution truly makes this book complete.

Lindsey Leavitt grew up in Las Vegas and now lives in Alabama with her husband and two small daughters. Although she has been a substitute teacher and a homecoming princess, she has never been a substitute princess—yet. She's still scanning the want ads. . . . Lindsey is currently hard at work on the next book in the Princess for Hire series.

Visit her online at www.lindseyleavitt.com